Starlight

Starlight

SCOTT ELY

WEIDENFELD & NICOLSON • *New York*

Published by Weidenfeld & Nicolson, New York
A Division of Wheatland Corporation
10 East 53rd Street
New York, NY 10022

Grateful acknowledgement is made for the following:

LITTLE WING by Jimi Hendrix. Copyright © 1968 and 1973 by Sea-Lark Enterprises, Inc. and Yameta Co., Ltd. All rights controlled by Unichappell Music, Inc. International Copyright Secured. ALL RIGHTS RESERVED. Used by permission.

PURPLE HAZE by Jimi Hendrix. Copyright © 1967 by Sea-Lark Enterprises, Inc. and Yameta Co., Ltd. All rights controlled by Unichappell Music, Inc. International Copyright Secured. ALL RIGHTS RESERVED. Used by permission.

THE WIND CRIES MARY by Jimi Hendrix. Copyright © 1967 and 1968 by Sea-Lark Enterprises, Inc. and Yameta Co., Ltd. All rights controlled by Unichappell Music, Inc. International Copyright Secured. ALL RIGHTS RESERVED. Used by permission.

BOLD AS LOVE by Jimi Hendrix. Copyright © 1968 by Sea-Lark Enterprises, Inc. and Yameta Co., Ltd. All rights controlled by Unichappell Music, Inc. International Copyright Secured. ALL RIGHTS RESERVED. Used by permission.

FOXY LADY by Jimi Hendrix. Copyright © 1967 and 1968 by Sea-Lark Enterprises, Inc. and Yameta Co., Ltd. All rights controlled by Unichappell Music, Inc. International Copyright Secured. ALL RIGHTS RESERVED. Used by permission.

VOODOO CHILD by Jimi Hendrix. Copyright © 1968 by Bella Godiva Music, Inc. and Chappell & Co., Inc. All rights controlled by Chappell & Co., Inc. International Copyright Secured. ALL RIGHTS RESERVED. Used by permission.

ALL ALONG THE WATCHTOWER by Bob Dylan. Copyright © 1968 by Dwarf Music. ALL RIGHTS RESERVED. International Copyright Secured. Reprinted by permission.

LIBRARY OF CONGRESS CATALOGING-IN-PUBLICATION DATA
Ely, Scott.
Starlight.

1. Vietnamese Conflict, 1961–1975—Fiction.
I. Title.
PS3555.L94S7   1987   813'.54   86-19058
ISBN 1-55584-047-7

Manufactured in the United States of America
Designed by Irving Perkins Associates, Inc.
First Edition 1987
10 9 8 7 6 5 4 3 2 1

To Carol

Starlight

CHAPTER

1

JACKSON WATCHED THE CHOPPER float in to land on the pad, the ship shimmering before his eyes in the heat waves, the rotors kicking up a cloud of red dust. Then the ship flew off, the pilot hugging the mountaintop to avoid exposing himself to fire from the NVA who owned the gorge below and the mountains into Laos. Tom Light walked out of the slowly settling dust cloud and stopped, turning in a slow circle as he looked over the firebase.

"Goddamn, why did he have to come here?" Jackson muttered, spitting to clear the taste of the red dust from his mouth. "The bad shit is on us now."

"Better stay clear of Light," Major Hale said.

"Nothing but fucking trouble where he goes," Jackson said.

"Goddammit, he won't stay here. Not at my firebase. He's going out in the bush."

Not unless Tom Light feels like going, Jackson thought. Hale liked to make threats he did not have the power to carry out. The men laughed at him behind his back.

Light was still on the pad, looking up at the sky like he was expecting the chopper to return. Jackson hooked his hands through his shoulder straps to ease the weight of the heavy radio he wore on his back and waited.

Jackson had heard all the stories. Light had at first been treated as an ordinary soldier, but the troops who went out with him had all died. Only Light survived a long list of ambushes: the Ia Drang Valley, Dak To, the Mang Yang Pass. Finally no one would go out with him, and the army made him a solitary sniper.

Three hundred days left. Now that bastard's here. I'll never be short, Jackson thought.

Light walked off the pad. His hair was clipped almost boot-camp short, and he was dressed in cut-off fatigues and an army-issue wool sweater. His legs were covered with jungle sores. Instead of boots he wore a pair of sandals made out of rubber tires.

His skin was unusually white, too white for a man who spent all his time under the tropical sun. Perhaps he had contracted a fungus during the rains, but that was hard to tell.

Light stood before them, cradling in a poncho what Jackson thought must be a rifle.

"What the fuck place is this?" Light asked in a tired voice.

"Desolation Row," Hale said.

"I'm supposed to be on R&R in Vung Tau," Light said to Hale. "Pilot who dropped me off said I could catch a chopper out here. Where is it?"

Jackson wondered what R&R was like for a man who walked the jungle alone for months at a time. Hale said Light lived off the land, ate snake jerky.

Hale took a step closer to Light and said, "Didn't they tell you at Two Corps?"

"They didn't tell me a fucking thing at Pleiku," Light replied in a slow, indifferent voice. "Got on a chopper at Pleiku. Thought we were headed for Vung Tau. I got my seven kills. They owe me."

"Orders say you come here," Hale said, talking fast like he always did when he got excited.

"Young trooper, will your radio reach Pleiku?" Light asked, turning to look at Jackson.

Jackson felt uncomfortable with Light's eyes on him. He shook his head and looked out across the green folds of the range the Montagnards called the Truong Son, the Long Mountains, into Laos. The mountains, most of them scarred with brown patches from napalm strikes, ran down the spine of Vietnam, some spurs running into the sea a hundred miles away.

Light continued, "We're up high. It'll reach."

"No way," Jackson said.

"It ain't that far," Light said.

Jackson looked over Light's shoulder at the green mountains.

Nothing out there, Jackson thought. A few abandoned Montagnard villages, the people relocated near Pleiku in planned villages built by the Americans. No roads. Just jungle and NVA. Not companies, divisions. The firebase had just one understrength battalion of two companies. Even fire support from the big 175-millimeter guns at Firebase Mary Lou ten miles away would not save them if the NVA attacked in strength. Only the threat of B-52 arclight strikes kept the NVA divisions in their sanctuaries in Laos.

"Put the whip on it and try," Light continued. "Major, tell your radio man to call me a chopper."

"Hold it, Jackson," Hale said. Then turning to Light, "I want you out in the bush now!"

"Call Two Corps back," said Light, his voice hard with anger. "Tell them they owe me a fucking R&R."

"Two of your kills were unconfirmed," Hale said. "You know the rules."

Both men stopped talking and stood watching each other like two dogs getting ready to fight. Hale, the shorter man, stood stiff-legged, raising himself on the toes of his jungle boots as he tried to stare down Light.

Although there were other radio telephone operators and communications specialists at the firebase, Jackson was Hale's personal RTO. Hale had a fear of being left without communications. During an operation near Saigon, he had become separated from his RTO, and the colonel in charge of the brigade had given Hale a poor efficiency report. That had kept him from becoming colonel.

"You're going out," Hale said.

"I'm going to Vung Tau," Light said.

"Then walk. You'll not ride a chopper out of my firebase. You'll not sleep here."

"I'll sleep on sheets in Vung Tau."

Hale hesitated, already beginning to back down.

Jackson hoped Light would not end up sleeping in the Tactical Operation Center. In the TOC, Jackson slept on a cot just outside Hale's cubicle. The men often asked Jackson if he was required to go to the latrine with the major. But he did not care what they said, for as long as he was Hale's RTO he could spend most of his three hundred days left in country in the safety of the TOC, the deepest bunker at the firebase. Hale often bragged he planned to make colonel without having to step outside the wire.

"I'm Two Corps here," Hale finally said, talking fast. "This firebase is my own little piece of hell. You do what I say."

Light unwrapped the poncho from around the rifle, a .303 instead of the standard issue M-16. The gray fiberglass stock was chipped and cracked in places, the larger cracks repaired with yellowish epoxy, and on the top was mounted a long, black starlight scope, the tube at the big end at least six inches in diameter. The barrel had been painted with a grainy, gray paint to match the stock.

This was the scope the Montagnards believed Light used to raise the dead, Jackson thought. But that was not surprising because the Yards believed that trees and rocks were inhabited by spirits. They sacrificed pigs to cure illnesses.

"You go out there," Light said, offering Hale the rifle.

"You're going to end up a stockade child, soldier!" Hale screamed, the veins standing out on his neck. "They'll lock you in a connex at Long Bien Jail, and I'll be a goddamn grandfather before they turn you loose! Get out there and hunt!"

"After my R&R," Light said.

"Now!" Hale shouted. And then in a lower voice, "I'll not have a mutiny over you like at Firebase Mary Lou."

"LBJ sounds OK by me," Light said in a bored voice as if they were discussing the next place he would spend an R&R.

"Soldier, don't you start fucking with the way I run this firebase. Get out there and kill the enemy."

"Not a fucking chance," Light said.

"Your mail's coming here now," Hale said. "Already got a letter for you. Two Corps told me you like to get mail regular. You won't get it staying here."

Light paused a moment and said, "I'll go in the morning. I want the letter before I leave."

"You'll have it," Hale said.

Then Light began to wrap up the rifle in the poncho. Hale stood and watched him.

Jackson knew Hale could not afford a mutiny. Duty at the firebase was his last chance. Hale kept a set of stateside colonel's insignia so he would be ready for the day when his promotion came through. Jackson sometimes had to polish the silver eagles.

"Be out of this camp by morning," Hale finally said, speaking slowly and clearly, emphasizing each word. "Don't come back without confirmation. You can raise me on your walkie-talkie."

"Goddamn, Major," Light said, "batteries go dead in a week. Heavy too. Threw the last one away."

"I want to log in bodies! I want to see them on this pad!" Hale yelled.

"They'll be here," Light said.

"They better. Jackson, take him to the ammo bunker. Then pick up his mail at the TOC. Get him a walkie-talkie. Stay with him. See he leaves before sunrise. If he's still here, you're going out with him. Give me the radio."

Hale walked off, puffs of red dust stirred by his boots, the radio slung over one shoulder. Soon the major would be in the TOC, protected by ten layers of packed sandbags from anything but a direct hit by a rocket.

Jackson began to gasp for air. Ever since childhood fear had produced this choking feeling, causing him to suck in great gulps of air. "Fish on the bank! Fish on the bank!" his friends at home in Alabama always chanted when they saw him do it.

"Calm down, young trooper," Light said. "You got good duty here."

But Jackson could not calm down. His eyes filled with tears at the strain of trying to breathe. With Light in camp the firebase was sure to take heavy incoming, and men were sure to die, those near Light in the most danger. That was why the men had mutinied at Firebase Mary Lou.

"I want to sleep," Light said. "Where's the bunker?"

Jackson did not reply. Then he felt Light's hand on his arm.

"Nothing's going to happen to you," Light said. "Show me where I sleep."

Jackson began to breathe easier.

"Over there," said Jackson, pointing to the mound of sandbags.

Jackson left Light at the ammo bunker and went to the TOC, returning with two cots, a walkie-talkie, and Light's letter. Light helped him take the cots down into the bunker. Stacked to the ceiling were cases of ammo and frags. There were also mortar shells, the willie peter stored upright to prevent the white phosphorous from settling to one side and causing the shell to pinwheel when it was fired. Once, CS riot-gas shells had been stored in the bunker, and the shells had leaked. Jackson's eyes watered slightly from the faint trace of gas that was left.

"I'd be thankful if you'd read me my letter," Light said, as they were unfolding the cots.

"I—" Jackson began.

Then it was happening again, the words refusing to come out. Jackson could hear nothing but the sound of air rushing into his lungs. He nodded his head.

"Just like the army," Light said, smiling for the first time since Jackson had met him. "Give a radio to a man who's too scared to talk."

"I'm not scared," Jackson said.

"Don't worry, you won't die today," Light continued. "Won't die tomorrow. You're safe with me."

"You don't know that," Jackson said.

"I know it like I know a man I put this scope on is gonna die," Light replied, tapping the poncho. "Now read me my letter."

Jackson read, "Dear Son, Brother Panky is so kind as to type this letter. He is praying for your safe return. Your mother's heart is better. He is praying for her too.

"The fishing has been good. I caught two hundred pounds of cats yesterday. Lost a new hoop net. Stolen, I think.

"Your mother says to tell you Ellen's new baby is fine. She is coming to see us soon.

"Your mother hopes you will make this the last year. Come home safe. Keep the Sabbath when you can. Brother Panky is praying for you. Your Daddy."

Light sat down on the cot and smiled at Jackson.

"Thanks, I'm going to sleep. You can write me a letter when I wake up," Light said.

Jackson went up and sat on the top step of the bunker. Light had said he would be safe, but he still would not have been surprised if the incoming had started falling.

Yet no attack came, and by late afternoon he had begun to believe Light's words. Quietly he went down the steps and in the semidarkness found Light asleep on a cot, the poncho-wrapped rifle by his side. The sniper smelled like the jungle, a scent of decaying leaves and damp earth. Jackson carefully walked close to Light and, crouching by the cot, touched the edge of Light's sweater. He wanted to touch Tom Light's arm or one of his bare legs but was afraid Light would awake.

"How do you do it?" Jackson whispered. "You could tell me. I could learn."

Jackson felt an impulse to shake Light awake and speak directly to the sniper but was stopped by his fear of the man. Light knew how to stay alive. It was not luck. Tom Light had long ago left luck far behind and attained a state beyond any fear of death. From where Light stood, the struggle to escape the net of the war must have seemed futile and without purpose.

As Jackson carefully stood up and left the bunker, he thought of going home. The commercial jet would lift off from Bien Hoa Air-base, and he would settle back against the soft seat, and as the cheers of the returning men died out, he would concentrate on watching a stewardess sashay down the aisle.

CHAPTER

2

JACKSON SAW A GROUP of soldiers walking across the compound toward the bunker, most of them from the mortar squad. Leander, the squad leader, walked in front while the others hung back. This was the mutiny Hale had been so worried about.

"Alabama, tell Light to come out," Leander said.

Jackson took several deep breaths and said, "He's asleep."

The men laughed. Leander took off his green NVA pith helmet with the single bullet hole above the left ear and wiped the sweat from his face, the red dust looking white against his black skin.

"Must be something wrong with the air," Leander said. "Calm down, Alabama, 'fore you choke to death."

Leander's audience laughed again. Jackson expected that from Leander who liked to run his mouth. More soldiers began to gather. Where was Hale?

"Tell that motherfucker Light to get up here. Or maybe we oughta drop a frag in there," Leander said.

Jackson started down the steps, but stopped when he saw Light come out of the bunker with his rifle. Light climbed the steps slowly, yawning as he went, blinking at the glare. Then he stood to face Leander and the men, standing there like a man might stand waiting for a bus in a large city, relaxed, indifferent to what was going on around him.

"We know you're bad," Leander said. "But you can't fight us all. We want you gone before you bring down the shit on us. Go back where you come from."

Light cradled the rifle in his arms and said nothing.

"You leave now," Leander continued.

The crowd murmured behind him.

"Get the fuck out of here!" a soldier yelled.

Two soldiers came out of the crowd. One was very thin and the other stocky with red hair and freckles. The thin soldier pretended his M-16 was a guitar. He fingered imaginary frets on the barrel with one hand while the other hand jumped about over the magazine and receiver.

The thin soldier sang, "Purple haze all around/Don't know if I'm coming up or down."

Everyone laughed, even Light and Leander.

"Fucking R&R'll blow Light away," someone yelled.

They were Reynolds & Raymond, speed freaks. Leander had named them R&R. Raymond talked nonstop, but no one had ever heard Reynolds speak except to sing Jimi Hendrix lyrics. Perhaps his silence was his way of mourning the guitarist's death. They had been attached to the mortar squad until Leander discovered they were always up on speed and refused to have them. Now they wandered about the firebase looking for something to steal so they could trade with the chopper crew chiefs for speed. The disappearance of C-rations, money, even a bore sight for the four-deuce mortars had been blamed on Reynolds & Raymond. Hale tolerated them because they were good fighters, fearless and crazy in battle.

"Hey, it's fucking Tom Light," Raymond said.

Reynolds played his M-16 behind his back.

"Let me borrow that starlight scope," Raymond said, reaching out to touch the scope.

Light swung the barrel of the rifle on Raymond's belly and said, "Get the fuck away from me."

"Go ahead, might as well shoot him now," Leander said. "He's as good as dead. We're all gonna get fucking wasted 'cause of you."

Reynolds & Raymond faded back into the crowd.

"Frag him," someone yelled.

"Those that have tried are dead," Light said in a calm voice.

No one in the crowd moved. Jackson realized they were trying to make up their minds which one of them would risk opposing that rifle.

Where was Hale? he thought.

Then Jackson saw Hale running across the compound carrying the radio.

"Goddamn, I told you there'd be trouble," Hale said to Light.

Light said, "I didn't start it."

"Put that fucking rifle down," Hale ordered.

"I got on a chopper for Vung Tau," Light said. "Didn't ask to come here."

"Ship his fucking ass out," Leander said.

"I'm in fucking command here," Hale shouted.

He looked at Leander and said, "Get rid of that gook helmet."

Jackson had heard Hale tell Leander that on a dozen occasions.

"Already got one hole in it. Bullets are like lightning. Don't strike twice in the same place," Leander said.

"Next time I see you there better be a steel pot on your head," Hale said.

Reynolds sang, "Footprints dressed in red/And the wind whispers Mary."

Everyone laughed.

"Shut that man up, Sergeant," Hale said to Leander.

"He don't belong to me," Leander said, not paying any attention to Hale's order.

Jackson noticed Reynolds looking at the starlight like it was made out of gold. Light glanced at him, and Reynolds backed off into the crowd again.

"Men, I made a bargain with Light," Hale said, talking fast. "He's leaving in the morning. Won't set foot on the firebase again. You have my word. Goddamn, Leander, see me in the TOC. That man Reynolds must be drunk. He'll be brought up on charges."

Again the men laughed.

"We are going to get the shit tonight because of him," Leander said, pointing at Light.

Light still had not lowered the rifle.

"Soldier, put that goddamn rifle down," Hale said. "You have my word nothing will happen to you."

"Don't need your word," Light said.

"Troops are gonna get wasted," Leander said.

"Shut the fuck up!" Hale yelled. "You open your mouth again and you're busted."

Leander continued to mutter to himself but not loud enough for Hale to make out the words.

"Move, all of you!" Hale yelled. "Bunched up like fucking sheep. One mortar round'd get you all."

"But it won't get Tom Light," Leander said to the men. "You'll be dead. He be back in the world doing any fucking thing he wants."

The men began to grumble among themselves. Light held up his hand for silence. They grew quiet.

Light said, "Starting right now, anybody comes fucking around this bunker is gonna die. Now get the fuck out of my sight. Bunch of goddamn base camp soldiers."

The crowd hesitated and then as if on a signal broke up, every man suddenly in a hurry to go somewhere else on the firebase. Only Leander and Reynolds & Raymond stayed.

"I'll get you, motherfucker," Leander said.

Light held the rifle and waited.

"Let me look through the starlight?" Raymond asked.

Reynolds played his M-16 with his teeth.

"Get out of here!" Hale yelled.

Then Leander left along with Reynolds & Raymond. Light lowered the rifle.

"Why can't you go now?" Hale asked.

"Because I've been out in the bush for two months," Light said. "I guess this is all the R&R I'm gonna get."

Hale said, "Jackson, you make sure he leaves. I'm holding you responsible."

Then Hale walked off toward the TOC.

Jackson started to gasp for breath and felt Light's hand on his shoulder.

"Calm down, young trooper. Nothing's gonna happen to you," Light said.

Jackson choked and gasped but gradually regained control. He thought of Leander's prediction, pictured how the mortar shrapnel would tear his body apart, and after it was over, Tom Light would still walk the bush alone.

CHAPTER

3

FROM THE TOP STEP of the bunker, Jackson watched the sun starting to sink behind the mountains, the light falling on the wire, the bunkers, the mortar tubes, and reflecting off the windshields of the ships on the pad. The whole firebase was bathed in a soft, golden glow utterly unlike the glare thrown down on the camp all day.

As the sun disappeared, the sky all red over Laos, Jackson heard an animal give a rasping call from the trees beyond the wire. Jackson took a deep breath. He feared the jungle, a wet, green, stinking place which could swallow up whole battalions of American infantry. But most of all he feared the enemy, who soon would begin probing the firebase's outer defenses, and the incoming which was sure to fall. Jackson heard Light coming up the steps.

"Young trooper, you ready to write?" Light said.

"In the bunker?" Jackson asked.

"That bunker's darker than the bottom of Moon Lake at midnight," Light said. "Won't be dark up here for awhile."

Jackson, breathing hard, looked out toward the mountains, the sky above them still faintly streaked with red. Light laughed.

"You won't die tonight. Now write like you promised," Light said.

16

Jackson took out the pen and paper and sitting on one of the steps below ground level waited for Light, who had taken a seat on the top step, to begin.

"Dear Daddy and Mama, I am fine and am glad Mama's heart is better," Light said. "There ain't much to do here in base camp. We all just sit around. Same old easy life. I hope Daddy finds out who stole his new hoop net. It will be spring soon, and the fishing will pick up, and he will have a good year. I have reenlisted. They gave me a $2,000 bonus. I had the army put it in the Greenville bank. You can draw it out anytime. This will be my last year here. I will come home. I will write again soon. Your son."

Light spoke the words without hesitation as if he had been thinking about the letter for a long time and had memorized what he wanted to say. The sniper was careful to pause at the end of each sentence to give Jackson time to write.

When Light signed the letter with a big scrawl, Jackson was reminded of the way he had written in elementary school. Jackson wrote a Mississippi address, a place called String Town, on the envelope.

"It's over on the Mississippi River," Light explained. "Daddy's a commercial fisherman."

Someone shot up a parachute flare over the perimeter, and they watched it drift out over the gorge, dropping white sparks, and slowly burn out, leaving the camp in darkness again.

"I can keep you alive," Light said.

Jackson felt like a wounded man watching a medevac approaching an LZ.

"Sooner or later that lifer Hale is gonna carry you out in the bush," Light continued. "I'll be watching. I'll take care of you. Write my letters. Daddy'll write his to you. That's all you have to do."

"Can I learn how you do it?" Jackson asked.

"Do what?"

"Stay alive."

"No, you can't learn. I'm the only one who knows about staying alive. Been doing it since Tet."

So Light was not going to teach him his secret, Jackson thought. But Light had promised to keep him alive. That was what mattered.

"How often will you be coming in?" Jackson asked.

"After seven kills," Light replied. "I don't want to wait that long. I promised Mama I'd write. If I don't, she'll worry. Won't help her heart. I want to know how she's doing. We'll meet out in the bush."

Jackson took one deep breath, thinking that he would not be able to breathe again. Light waited patiently for him to speak.

"I'm not going out there," Jackson finally said after what seemed to him like a long time, aware that Light was pretending not to notice that he was gasping for air.

"I can't do much for you here," Light said. Then he laughed softly. "But out in the bush 'less you step on a cobra snake or a tiger eats you, harm won't come to you," he continued. "I guarantee it."

"Be dead just the same," Jackson said, who did not think the threat of tigers or cobras was funny.

"I told you I'll keep you alive. Before I'm out there a week, the dinks'll be scared shitless of me. I work at night with the starlight. No more to it than spotlighting deer."

"Why should I go out there? I'll get blown away."

"I already told you. When the major goes out in the bad bush, you go with him. But if you write my letters, I'll look after you. Keep you alive."

"I'll take the chance he won't go."

"He'll go. Lifers can't make rank sitting in camp. We'll pick us a frequency. Every night after it gets dark, set the radio and wait."

"Major Hale won't let me out of the wire."

"Volunteer for a listening post. Tell him you're itching to see the shit. Remember, without me you're gone. Wait until after tonight. You'll see. They'll hit us tonight and men'll die. I saw it in the starlight. I'll keep you alive."

"How did you see?"

"I saw it."

He's crazy and so am I for listening to him, Jackson thought.

"You'll get me wasted," Jackson said.

But as Jackson spoke he wished he could have the words back, for Light's face had gone rigid.

"Young trooper, you can't spend the war panting like a worn-out hound every time a little incoming falls," Light said in the same tone he had used in his argument with Hale.

"I got a right to be scared," Jackson said.

"Being scared'll kill you quick as not giving a shit," the sniper said.

Then off on the ridge below the camp Jackson saw a flash followed by the fiery trail of a rocket. "Rocket!" someone shouted. Jackson heard the men running for the bunkers. He started down the steps.

"No need for that," Light said.

Jackson paid no attention to Light, but then he felt Light's hand on his arm.

"Sit," Light said.

And crouching on the steps, gasping for breath, Jackson watched the rocket fall near the TOC, followed by an explosion that shook the firebase.

"See, you're safe as a rabbit in the briars," Light said.

"We've been hit with rockets before," Jackson said.

"I knew it wasn't going to hit us," Light said. "You won't ever know."

And Light was right, Jackson thought to himself. He had never known. Light knew.

"I'm going to sleep. Don't sleep much out in the bush. Why this place is better than a weekend in Memphis," Light said.

Jackson sat on the other cot in the dark and listened to Light's slow, regular breathing. Then the camp began to take mortar rounds, and Jackson heard the thump of the incoming and the replying fire from the firebase's mortars. Jackson discovered to his amazement that he was breathing easy for the first time during an attack. Light slept soundly through it all.

After the attack was over, he decided to take a look at the rifle, especially the starlight scope Light used to predict the attack.

But maybe Light had only guessed that the firebase would take rounds as it did every night. That was a prediction everyone at the firebase made each night, that incoming would fall on someone else. Yet Light had survived all the ambushes and firefights when other men had died, and the trick to it might be in the scope, a secret Light wanted to keep to himself.

Carefully shielding the flashlight with his hand, he walked over to the cot where Light was sleeping on his side with his back to the rifle.

As Jackson unwrapped the poncho, he kept one eye on Light who still slept peacefully. But as he lifted the rifle off the cot, Light rolled over on his back. Jackson froze, waiting for the sniper's blue eyes to pop open. Muttering something, Light rolled back over and returned to a deep sleep.

Jackson took the rifle and went up out of the bunker. All the stars were out, but there was no moon. That was OK. The scope would gather enough light to work. He switched on the scope, put the rifle to his shoulder, and pressed his eye to the neoprene eyepiece, the rubber making the scope smell like the snorkeling mask he used at Pensacola every summer. Though the camp was in complete darkness, he could see everything: bunkers, the guard tower, a soldier at a piss tube, all with a green, undersea tint, little sparkles of white light playing around the edges of the outlines.

Mortar rounds began to fall on the firebase again. Flares went up and Jackson turned the scope on one. The glare blinded him. A round hit very close and shrapnel whistled overhead. But he was afraid to move until he could see. He flattened himself out against the sandbags and tried to focus his eyes, gasping for breath. Sparkles of green and purple light appeared before his eyes. He could imagine his death clearly, one round falling on his head, then nothing.

When he could see again, he crawled back down into the bunker. He struggled to breathe, sitting with his back against the wall of the bunker and pressing his hands to his chest. Suddenly the big end of the scope began to glow and an image formed as if on a TV screen.

More rounds began to fall, but mesmerized by the green glow of the scope, he remained on the steps trying to make out the image through the dust.

In the scope a soldier Jackson had never seen before walked on a jungle trail. As the soldier stepped over a fallen log, he disappeared in the smoke of an explosion. A mine. Then the image faded and was gone, leaving Jackson gasping for breath and wondering if he had seen anything at all.

The rounds stopped falling. He went down into the bunker and wrapped the rifle back up in the poncho. This time Light did not stir, asleep on his stomach, one arm dangling off the edge of the cot, his breathing smooth and even.

Later Jackson went to sleep in his flak jacket, expecting to be awakened by another attack. He woke suddenly, but there was no thump of incoming. Light's wooden cot frame creaked, and he realized Light was awake. Pointing the flashlight toward the sound, he saw Light sitting crosslegged on the cot, cleaning the rifle that lay scattered in pieces about him.

"Turn that goddamn thing off!" Light said.

Jackson switched off the flashlight.

"What'd you see in it, young trooper?" Light asked.

Jackson thought about lying but decided against it. Again he found he could not speak, listening to the heavy sound of his own breathing. He could not see Light.

"Talk, goddamn you!" Light said.

"The bunkers, the wire," Jackson said, the words coming out in a rush.

"What else?"

"Nothing."

"What the fuck did you see?"

The C-rations Jackson had eaten that evening tried to rise out of his stomach, but although he tasted bile, he managed to keep them down. There was nothing to stop Light from killing him for touching the rifle.

"A green light," Jackson said.

"That all, just green light?" Light asked. "Didn't see troops getting blown away? They're gonna die all right. You saw them in the starlight."

"I didn't see anything," Jackson said.

Click, click, click, came a sound from the cot, and Jackson realized that Light was reassembling the rifle in the dark and doing it faster than Jackson had ever imagined possible. Now that Jackson's eyes had adjusted to the darkness he could see movement from Light's cot, but no shape he could say for sure was an arm or a leg.

"This ain't a cheap ass M-16," Light said. "Every part is milled, not stamped."

He heard a series of clicks which meant Light was running a round through the action and then the single, sharp click as the firing pin came forward to strike an empty chamber.

"Weird through the starlight, ain't it?" said Light.

Jackson decided to say nothing.

"When you look at the dinks through the scope, they look like men shined up on a wall with a green carbide lantern," Light continued. "And sometimes I see things through it I'd just as soon not. What'd you see?"

Light was not much older than him, but Jackson had a feeling Light was ancient. He talked old.

"Nothing. Just green light." Jackson said. "I'm not as dumb as the Yards. You raised any dead soldiers with it lately?"

"I might as well talk to a sandbag as to you," Light said. "I thought you were smart,"

"I didn't see—" Jackson began.

"Maybe you didn't," Light said, cutting him off. "One of these nights you will. Then we can talk." Then Light continued, "Remember, set your radio long about sundown every day. Don't you forget."

"How will I find you?" Jackson asked.

"I saw a big rock up on the ridge when I was flying in today. That'll be the place."

"They'll kill me. Hale don't even like to send recon out there.

The air force has napalmed the shit out of it, and the dinks haven't left.''

"Dinks won't touch you. I promise. Just remember, you'll be out there anyhow with the major before it's over. Without me you're a dead man. You coming out?''

Maybe Light knew, Jackson thought. Maybe Light could watch the pictures in the scope and tell who was going to die.

Jackson took a deep breath and said, "I'll be there,'' but thinking at the same time, Goddamn war, fucking crazy Tom Light.

"Calm down, young trooper,'' Light said. "You'll be shooting dinks through the starlight 'fore long.''

Jackson lay down on the cot and tried to go to sleep, listening to a series of clicks as Light ran another round through the action.

CHAPTER

4

JACKSON OFTEN CLIMBED the guard tower next to the TOC and through a pair of glasses watched the men at the engineer camp completing the final circle of wire around their perimeter. The men called the mountain on which the engineer camp was built Little Tit and the mountain they lived on Big Tit while the narrow valley between the two was known as the Cunt. Sometimes, as he stood in the tower, he imagined that he was atop a gigantic reclining woman who lay with her head in Laos and her legs stretching toward the South China Sea.

When he tired of watching the engineers, he turned the glasses toward Laos. As he looked at the green mountains, their outlines indistinct in the haze of the dry season, he often thought of Tom Light who was wandering through the jungle somewhere on the woman. Already he had accumulated a stack of letters from Mississippi, the addresses on the envelopes neatly typed.

In the ammo bunker that morning he had awakened before dawn and turned the flashlight on Light's empty cot. The guards at the gate and on the perimeter had not seen Light leave, and the pilots swore they had not taken him out by chopper. No one at the outpost ever mentioned Light's name. At night he would set the radio on

24

the frequency they had agreed on and wait for Light to call, but so far had heard nothing.

Every day the patrols went out, mostly into the Cunt, on search-and-destroy missions. Sometimes they found caches of rice or weapons, but they seldom brought back a body.

Before Jackson had become Hale's RTO he had been assigned to Captain Wilson, Hale's intelligence officer who was dead now, killed by a mine. He helped Wilson search the bodies of any enemy who were brought in. There were never many, at the most one or two a week. Jackson got used to the smell of feces and blood and burned flesh, but he never liked going through their pockets. Wilson was after letters, copies of orders.

Wilson usually sat beneath a parachute someone had rigged up to make some shade and waited for Jackson to bring him the documents. The captain always called them documents. Jackson remembered one man in particular. The patrols had not killed anyone for ten days, and all Hale could talk about was body count. Finally the chopper brought in the body of a young NVA soldier and dropped it on the pad.

Jackson stretched the man out, straightening one shattered leg. Then he went through the soldier's front pockets. When Jackson rolled the soldier over to go through his back pockets, it was like the man was a rubber sack filled with water, heavy and hard to handle. Then Jackson searched the back pockets and found a picture wrapped in clear plastic of a small child. She stood on a stretch of green grass with trees behind her. Probably a park. The child held a white flower. A lotus?

"Found some documents?" Wilson asked.

He took Wilson the picture. Wilson looked at it a moment and put it in his pocket. Jackson wanted to smash him in the face.

"Strip him. Might have some more documents concealed on him," Wilson said.

Jackson returned to the body and finished the job but found nothing.

As he thought of the picture, Jackson wondered if Light took dead men's pictures out and looked at them.

Jackson always carried the radio because the ability to talk with the TOC anytime he wished made him feel secure. Radio men were often shot first in ambushes, but since Hale seemed determined to avoid going out in the field, Jackson felt safe for the present. Hale spent most of his time in the TOC working on his maps. And if the major did go out, Jackson believed he could count on Light's promise of protection.

Sometimes he set the radio on a frequency assigned to the platoons and listened to the lieutenants talk to Hale in the TOC. During firefights he heard the fear in the voices of the young officers and their RTOs.

On clear nights he put on the whip and climbed up in the tower to talk with operators as far away as Qui Nhon on the coast. He wondered if with the addition of a longer whip he might be able to talk with Saigon or even Australia. There were even nights when he considered the possibility of reaching home. A chain of ham operators around the world might be able to patch him through to his parents or his girl who had taken a job in Birmingham.

"Loretta, Loretta," he found himself saying one night into the handset as he thought about the girl, standing by himself in the darkness.

Static came out of the handset.

It was crazy, he thought to himself.

But he said it again, "Loretta, Loretta."

Jackson promised himself he would never try it again. He did not want to come home from the war crazy.

At the firebase there was constant speculation about what the engineers had been sent up to the Laotian border to do. Some thought it was to build a road connecting the firebase with Pleiku while others claimed they were certain that the engineers were going to build an airbase in the Cunt.

One morning Hale assembled the two companies, Alpha and Charlie, and all speculation ended. Jackson with the radio strapped to his back stood next to Hale who had an M-16 cleaning rod in his hand. A big piece of plywood was nailed to a couple of two-byfours behind him. Whatever was on it was covered with a section of parachute.

"Men, our mission is to protect those engineers," Hale began.

They stood beneath the hot sun and waited for Hale to get around to whatever he was going to talk about. And Hale stood before them looking down at the ground as if he was having difficulty deciding what he was going to say next. The men, sensing his nervousness, began to whisper among themselves.

"The engineers are here to build a fence," Hale finally continued.

He nodded to two sergeants who pulled back the parachute to reveal a map.

"It's going to start here," he said, pointing to a spot on the big map which Jackson recognized as the Cunt.

He paused again, looking up at the high blue sky like he wished a voice would come out of it and finish his speech for him. Then his audience would have to believe. The major took a deep breath.

"We're going to fence every valley so the NVA can't infiltrate into Two Corps," Hale said, talking fast, tracing with the pointer the path of the fence on the map. "That fence could change the whole course of the war. If the NVA can't get into 'Nam there'd be no war. Then we'd just have to fight Charlie. We kicked his ass during Tet. We'll do it again."

Everyone was silent.

Then Raymond said, "That's a fucking great idea, Major. Fence those bastards out!"

And Reynolds sang, "There must be some kind of way out of here/Said the joker to the thief."

"Make it a big fence. Ten foot tall. Fucking little dinks'll never climb it," Raymond continued. "Me and my buddy Reynolds will be proud to help."

Reynolds continued to play his M-16.

"They're fucked up again on speed," a sergeant said to Hale.

"Goddammit! How're they getting drugs? Get'em out of here," Hale said.

Everyone laughed, and the sergeant led Reynolds & Raymond away.

"That goddamn fence is going up on schedule!" Hale shouted.

"Bullshit!" Leander shouted, the pith helmet pulled down low over his eyes.

Now a kind of collective growl came from the battalion, and Jackson, who was standing behind Hale, wondered if he was watching the beginnings of a mutiny.

Hale said, "I know what you men are thinking. You can frag me and my officers."

One of the lieutenants flinched at the mention of the word frag.

"The brass at Two Corps wants this fence," Hale continued. "It's going up."

"Yeah, it'll go up. You'll make colonel. We'll all get fucking wasted!" Leander yelled.

"I see you one more time with that goddamn gook helmet on, and you're busted," Hale said.

"You're gonna see plenty of these fucking helmets," Leander said.

Everyone laughed.

"Leander, the only way you or anybody else is going to get off Desolation Row is to build that fence," Hale said. Then he paused and continued, talking fast, "I'm going to tell you men why we're going to build that goddamn fence. They wouldn't tell you why in the Russian army. Remember that. Some general at Two Corps has a son-in-law who's in the chain-link fence business in Chicago. This goddamn civilian son-in-law got himself a contract for one thousand miles of interstate highway fence. Paid off some congressman. But didn't pay off the right one or pay enough because he lost the bid on the contract. Got himself stuck with all that goddamn fence. Daddy the general found a way to take care of his own. Goddamn, men, a two-star general can do any fucking thing he wants!"

No one laughed.

"You mean some asshole general is gonna fence the dinks out of 'Nam with a fucking playground fence?" Leander yelled. "That dude is crazy."

That set everyone to laughing. Hale patiently waited for them to stop.

Jackson wondered what he could do to escape Hale. He could ask to be transferred, but that might mean he would end up as a rifleman in some company that stayed out in the bush for months at a time, far away from Light's protection. With an extra long whip he might be able to reach Saigon and tell the commander of American forces what the general was trying to do. Or better yet he might have his signal relayed to the states by ham operators. Jackson tried to remember the chain of command, those pictures he had seen in company orderly rooms ever since basic training. The Joint Chiefs could be told or even the President. He imagined the Secretary of the Army flying into II Corps and relieving the general of his command.

The men were quiet and Hale was talking again as Jackson returned from his reverie of escape.

"We're going to fence this country all the way down to the goddamn South China Sea!" Hale said, speaking very fast. "It's going to work. We can't go up to Hanoi and kill'em all. The politicians won't let us fight this war. Fence'em out! Put a mile of cleared ground on either side of the fence and kill any goddamn thing in it that moves. The commies did it in Europe. We can do it here. It'll be a goddamn chain-link curtain!"

No one laughed, and Jackson realized it was because the men knew they were trapped.

"Those hard-core NVA won't let that fence go up without a fight. They're sitting in Holiday Inn base camp right now over there in Laos waiting to see what we're going to do. They probably already know if those goddamn sorry ARVNs are in on this," Hale continued.

Jackson had heard of Holiday Inn base camp. Once, two battalions had been sent to attack it, and only parts of them had returned back across the border. Soon after he had arrived at the outpost a rumor had started that they were going into Laos after it. He had been unable to eat or shit until he had discovered that they were not going after all.

"One of these days we may have to go over there again," Hale said. "This time we'll run'em all the way back up to Hanoi!"

Now Hale had become very excited, waving his arms about to emphasize his words.

Jackson wished he was out in the bush with Light. Once work on the fence started the builders and their defenders would be easy targets for the NVA. He hoped Hale would not decide to go down there to direct the defense personally.

"I know you've heard stories about that base camp. The NVA are tough. They're hard-core," Hale said. "But you can be just like them. Men, back in high school, out in the piny woods of Louisiana, I used to play football for a coach named Hog Willis. Goddamn, but we loved that man. Hated him too because he worked us. Made us mean. Hog got his name from catching razorbacks barehanded down in Honey Island Swamp. Wrestled'em down and tied'em up with barbed wire. Coach hunkered down with those hogs in the mud. You got the hunker down with the goddamn NVA! What will it be men? Are you going to let the enemy run us off this mountain?"

"Hell, no, Sir!" one of the lieutenants shouted.

Hale looked hard at the men, waiting for them to take up the yell. But they were silent, most of them staring down at their boots. Even Leander had nothing to say. Hale dismissed the battalion.

Jackson wished he could call for a chopper on the radio and fly away from Hale and the fence and the war and Light. Fly home to the farm: fields and pond and pasture and woods and the white frame house where he could sleep safe in his bed and wake to the sound of a mockingbird singing its heart out, not to the thump of incoming walking heavy across the compound.

CHAPTER

5

DURING THE NEXT FEW WEEKS SHIPMENTS of wire, steel poles, and concrete started arriving at the engineer camp, brought up from Pleiku by the big helicopters, the sky cranes. Jackson thought the sky cranes looked like huge wasps bringing food back to their nests, the cargo dangling between their long legs on steel cable. Gradually a mountain of wire began to grow at the camp until it seemed to him that there was not going to be room for the men.

He thought they might start stringing just outside the perimeter, but instead they began down in the Cunt. One morning the radio operator in the TOC told him that the air force was sending a plane to drop a 1,000-pound bomb to clear out the initial landing zone in the jungle. He went up to the tower and waited with the guard. Soon the plane appeared, flying so high it was just a speck in the blue sky. When it reached the mountain it made a turn and circled the Cunt.

Jackson watched through armored glasses the plane's slow circle over the Cunt, hoping he would be able to see the bomb fall. But the explosion took him by surprise, the tower guard tapping him on the shoulder and pointing down into the Cunt where a cloud of red dust rose silently, the deep roar reaching them in a few seconds later. Using the LZ as a base, the engineers with chainsaws, TNT, bulldozers, Rome plows, and thousands of gallons of defoliant attacked the jungle, creating a red scar on the Cunt. Then they started stringing wire.

Hale placed platoons in permanent positions at the LZ, rotating fresh ones into it every week. The engineers were choppered back to Little Tit each night. But work on the fence went slowly, the NVA sappers blowing up at night what the engineers had built during the day.

When the platoons were back at the firebase the men lived with rats in underground bunkers. After dark the big gray animals had no fear of the men, and some who had developed a taste for tobacco ate cigarettes out of the pockets of sleeping men, leaving only the filters. In their spare time they held rat-killing contests, shooting the animals with pistols. Someone had the chopper pilots bring up a cat from Pleiku, but the rats, some which were almost as big as the cat, cornered it in the ammo bunker one night and killed it.

"Alabama, you get Light to bring you a tiger in from the bush, waste these fucking rats," a soldier said to Jackson one day.

"I got a cat at home that'll take care of those rats," Jackson said. "Gook cats are just like the ARVNs, no fucking good."

"Shit, Alabama, you'd need a pack of cats. Call Light up on that radio you sleep with and tell him to get us a tiger," the soldier said.

"He's using them like tracking dogs to hunt down the dinks. Can't spare any," Jackson replied.

The soldier and his friends laughed. Jackson liked the attention, but no one got too close. They were afraid of Light. Jackson had spent the night in the bunker with Light and lived.

"We know it's gonna happen," a soldier finally told him. "No sense one of us getting wasted when you get blown away."

And Jackson realized he would have done the same had he been in their place.

Jackson had watched Desolation Row go up in one day. At dawn the air force hit the mountaintop with 250-pound bombs. Then the helicopters inserted a platoon which encountered light resistance from the NVA, who chose to pull back and drop mortars in on the mountaintop. Jackson had been a member of that first platoon and had watched most of his squad die, killed by mortars. Engineers followed with chainsaws, and cut down the trees. Once a secure LZ was formed, a bulldozer was brought in by sky crane to finish the job of clearing the trees and leveling the ground.

A chopper brought in a 20-foot prefabricated steel tower and dropped it at the center of the LZ. The engineers tied a rope to the tower and used it to mark the circumference of a circle with a 250-foot radius. The bulldozer finished the job of clearing brush and trees out of the way. Then helicopters came and dropped concertina wire which the men strung on metal stakes in a pyramid pattern, two rows on the bottom and one on top. After that the choppers dropped sections of perforated steel plate and cratering charges at 20-foot intervals around the circumference of the circle. The men used the charges to blow holes for bunkers and the plate to provide support for overhead cover made out of sandbags. Mortars were brought in, two 81-millimeter tubes for illumination and three 4.2-inch mortars for close fire support. Jackson worked hard on his bunker and spent a sleepless night with three other soldiers staring out into the jungle, waiting for the ground attack that never came.

In the morning Hale arrived with the 105 howitzers, each gun brought in as a single load by a chopper. The howitzers were formed into three double emplacements. Recoilless rifles were put in position. A communications center bunker was built which would be the TOC and a fire support coordination bunker was constructed. Radar emplacements were installed on the perimeter along with searchlights. Rocket-propelled grenade screens of chain-link fence were set in place over the bunkers.

Two more circles of concertina wire were added. The men placed claymore mines along with trip wires attached to flares and booby traps. From the wire they hung beer cans filled with pebbles. It did not seem possible to Jackson that a man could get through the wire, but he had been told stories of NVA sappers dressed only in loincloths who could effortlessly pick their way through the tangle.

Machine-gun emplacements were periodically shifted to prevent the enemy from gaining a fix on them. Every night the men planted claymore mines in new locations just behind the first circle of wire. And small patrols of four or five men and sometimes single men were placed on listening posts out in the bush.

Soon after Jackson arrived Hale had ordered the men to plant electronic listening devices outside the wire. These responded to vibrations by producing a beep on a set of headphones worn by an operator in the TOC. But this plan was abandoned when it was discovered that small animals, the wind, and the mortar firing produced vibrations which were picked up by the sensors.

One night the operator, an Indian from New Mexico named Alfred Ten Deer, had thrown the headphones down after hours of trying to distinguish beeps produced by enemy movement from the others and had declared he preferred going back out in the bush to spending another second on the headphones.

"Goddamn ping-ping inside my head," Alfred had said, holding his hands over his ears after he had thrown the headphones against the wall of the bunker.

Within the circle of wire there were ammo dumps, stores of C-rations, and an aid station. All supplies were flown in by chopper. Mail came every day, and once a week a chaplain flew out to hold services for those men who were interested.

Sometimes the mess sergeant at Pleiku sent them hot food on the choppers in mermite cans during a lull in the fighting. In the insulated containers was the same old army food that he had grown used to eating in the States. Most of the time they ate C-rations. Once, Jackson ended up with five straight meals of ham and beans, food that tasted terrible, making it impossible to trade for fruit cocktail or spaghetti. Sometimes they got a case of dehydrated rations. Jackson liked the chicken and rice.

Every day was the same, clear and hot. They were given beer, but it was always hot. Jackson would have given a month's pay for a cold beer. There was plenty of drinking water but not enough for showers. One day Hale had fifty-five-gallon drums of water flown in and a shower rigged up using a drum with holes punched in the bottom. Everyone got to lather up and rinse off. Later they built a permanent water tank, the water heated with a diesel fuel fire. For a few days they all took hot showers until the NVA took out the water tank with a lucky shot from a 122-millimeter rocket.

Jackson knew it could have been much worse for him. He could be an RTO for one of the lieutenants stationed in the Cunt. One lieutenant had already lost three radio men. But Jackson wished he was back at one of the big base camps in Pleiku or, better yet, Cam Ranh Bay where they had movies, swimming pools, ice cream, and passes into town.

Gradually the NVA began to step up their rocket and mortar attacks on both the engineer camp and the firebase, although except for probes by small squads of NVA, there had been no ground attacks. If a ground attack against the firebase came, it would have to be launched along a long ridge that connected the mountaintop with the rest of the chain. This was the place where he was to meet with Light when Light contacted him on the walkie-talkie. Although he set the radio on Light's frequency every night, Jackson had heard nothing from him.

The intensity of the attacks increased, and Jackson sat in the TOC listening to the incoming, the dust from the sandbags above his head sifting down on him as each shell or rocket exploded in the compound. Although he was afraid, he did not believe he would die. He had moved the cot Light had slept on into the TOC. Pressing his nose against the canvas fabric of the cot he tried to remember how Light had smelled, that stink of decaying leaves and damp earth.

"You promised. Goddamn, you promised," he often whispered into the canvas.

After the attack was over he would lie on the cot, just outside the circle of light thrown by the TOC's single naked bulb, and think of home.

I could have gone to college, he often thought. I could have had a deferment.

But Jackson found it difficult to take the deferment. Jackson's great-grandfather had ridden with Forrest, his grandfather had fought at Belleau Wood, his father in Normandy, and his uncle Frank in Korea. He had noticed how excited his father and Frank got when they watched the war on the news, the camera bouncing around all over the place when the action got hot. They expected him to enlist.

The summer he graduated from high school he began to help his uncle Frank at the cleanup shop for used cars. Then it was fall, and some of his friends went off to college while others were drafted. He polished cars with a buffer in the shop and waited.

"It won't last much longer," Frank said. "You're going to miss it."

"Mama wants me to go to college," Jackson said.

"You can go after. Sure, I know you're worried now. You'll be all right."

Frank had been the one who had cured him of his fear of hand-grabbing for catfish. Every spring he had dreaded the sound of the first heavy rain falling on the roof because that meant the lake would soon flood the woods and fields.

On Saturday mornings his father and Frank would take him to the backwaters and force him to wade through the flooded trees and brush and stick his hand down into that cold, muddy water to grope about for a fish under a submerged log or in a hollow tree trunk.

There was a trick to it he just couldn't seem to learn. He always got finned by the fish or ended up with a turtle and a few times with a snake or, worse yet, grabbed the fish's tail and the cat, twisting its cold, slick body out of his grip, escaped.

Finally in disgust they allowed him to stay in the boat. Then one day Frank had made him get out of the boat and taking his hand showed him how to place it gently on the fish, both their hands under the log together, he smelling the whiskey on his uncle's breath.

"Feel him, boy?" Frank asked. "Pretend it's a woman. Tickle her, find out where she lives."

His father and Frank had laughed.

But suddenly he had understood, not because he knew anything about touching a woman. He understood because Frank had said the right words, had showed him. Closing his hand around the fish's tail, he jerked the cat out from under the log.

Maybe Frank was right about the war, Jackson thought. Maybe I should enlist.

But instead he waited, and Frank kept telling him about the good times he had had in Korea. Frank showed him the leather holster and pistol taken off a North Korean officer he had shot in a night ambush.

But Jackson's mother had other ideas.

"None of my family ever went to college, no Jackson either. Bill's going," his mother kept saying every time Frank mentioned the war.

And his father said, "I told him I'd pay. He says he don't want to go."

So Jackson worked on the cars and looked after the cows and made sure the five thousand chickens in the three big chicken houses had plenty of feed and water while his father drove off to work fifty miles away at the steel plant in Birmingham.

On weekends he and Loretta went to the movies and afterwards went to the old Jackson homesite to make love in his pickup. Years ago there had been a fire. Now only the foundation, the well, and the jonquils remained.

He remembered one night they had driven out to the homesite. Loretta had just found a job in Birmingham as a legal secretary.

"Maybe we should get married?" he said. "I could find a job working on cars in Birmingham."

"You're going to be drafted," she said.

"You could come live with me after basic."

"You'll be going to Vietnam."

"Maybe I'll get Germany."

Her clothes were gone, and he reached out for her. She pushed his hand away.

"Are you going to spend the rest of your life fixing up cars?" she asked.

"You know I'm waiting on the draft," he said.

"Go to college."

"Frank's teaching me the business."

"You don't want to marry me."

She began to dress. After that he still took her to the movies occasionally, but they no longer went to the homesite.

Then Jackson got the letter. He was relieved someone had made up his mind for him.

In late October he and his father went to the river near the homesite. At the churchyard across the river, the cavalryman and the marine lay buried. They fished for bass, wading the shoals. At noon they stopped for lunch on a large, flat boulder in the center of the steam. They gutted the fish, throwing the entrails into the river. Jackson washed the blood off his hands in the cold water.

"Were you afraid?" Jackson asked.

"Sometimes, mostly before we fought," his father said. "Once it started I was all right. You'll be all right too. Jacksons have always been good soldiers."

"Did you hate the men you killed."

"They were Kraut bastards. They killed my buddies. I hated them during the war but not after. They were soldiers like me."

"I don't hate the Viet Cong."

It was funny, Jackson thought. He had imagined he would be fighting little men dressed in black pajamas, not NVA regulars.

"You'll learn," his father said.

But he had not learned to hate them. He would kill them if he could, but it was hard to hate men who had been trapped by the war the same as he.

When he came home on leave after basic, Loretta showed up at Frank's shop. Jackson was steam cleaning an engine.

"I'm thinking about moving to Birmingham," she said.

"When?"

"You'll be gone."

"This time next year I'll be home."

"You be careful."

He put down the steam hose and kissed her. Then he drove her home.

And in the bunker at night he often tried to picture his homecoming, his parents and uncles, and Loretta meeting him at the Birmingham Airport. But one night he closed his eyes and found it impossible to imagine what Loretta looked like.

"Loretta, Loretta," he said out loud, hoping the words could make her appear.

But all he could imagine was the figure of a girl without a face. He knew if he did not have her picture wrapped in plastic in a pocket of his fatigue jacket he would never be able to summon up her green eyes and red hair, her knees skinned from playing softball.

But one person whose image was always clear in his mind, whom he was able to call up anytime he wished, was Light. All he had to do was close his eyes and there was Light with his skin that was too white, his washed-out blue eyes, his face set in an expression that gave no clue to what he was thinking.

Then Jackson wondered where Light was and wished that he was with him, sleeping out in the jungle wrapped in a poncho against the cool night air of the mountains, safe from the incoming, safe from the NVA because the enemy feared Light like death itself. At the end of his tour he would go home and in a few weeks images of the firebase and mountains and Hale and even Light would fade away to be lost forever, for he would carry home no pictures of them.

CHAPTER

6

JACKSON HAD JUST SET THE RADIO on Tom Light's frequency when Light's voice, the words spoken in a whisper, came out of the handset. Jackson was sitting on the TOC's overhead cover and had attached the whip to the radio because he had feared that Light might have wandered far over into Laos and out of range.

"I've been killing, but they're too proud to give up their dead. Nothing to show the major yet," Light said.

There was a long pause before Light spoke again.

"Some nights I don't want to look in the scope. See strange stuff. Know what I mean?"

Static crackled out of the handset.

Gasping for breath, Jackson pressed the transmission bar but could say nothing, thinking of what he had seen in the scope that first night.

"Goddamn you, talk," Light said.

"Come in," Jackson said.

"I can't come in," Light said. "I can't never come in. Can't go home."

"What about me? You promised."

40

"You're going home. I gave my word. Meet me tomorrow night at the rock."

"I've never been out there. I don't know how."

"It'll be just like walking down the street in Saigon. I won't let nothing happen to you."

And Jackson believed Light's promise, thinking that he was safer out in the bush with Light than in the TOC. At that moment, Jackson thought, an NVA soldier might be humping the rocket or mortar shell down the Ho Chi Minh Trail that was meant for him.

In the morning Jackson went to see Hale who was down in the TOC working at his map tripod.

"Sir, I'd like to go out on a listening post tonight," Jackson said, taking several deep breaths to try to calm himself.

"Why's that?" Hale said. "I need you here."

"I want to know—" Jackson began, realizing that Hale was probably wondering how he could talk and gasp for air at the same time. "I want to know what it's like out there."

Hale laughed and said, "Stick close to me. Don't want my RTO wandering around in the bush." Then he patted Jackson on the shoulder. "I'm going to run this operation from down here. I've been out there. This is my third goddamn tour. Go out and the dinks'll blow you away."

"I want to go out," Jackson said.

"You're staying with me. I go out, then you go. Not until." Then Hale continued, "Go plot those patrol positions for tonight."

Stay close to Hale and get fucked, Jackson thought as he went to the map. I want to stay close to Tom Light. I'm going out if I have to crawl through the fucking wire.

That night, his face painted with camouflage and carrying Light's letters inside his fatigue jacket, Jackson walked out the front gate on wobbly legs, concentrating on taking slow, even breaths. No one at the gate had questioned him. He carried the radio so he could call the TOC when he started back in and tell them he was coming. Light had promised nothing about protecting him from friendly fire.

He had considered what would happen if Hale discovered he had disobeyed orders. The major had just gone to sleep when he left, and Jackson hoped to find Light, write his letter, and return before Hale woke up. But if the NVA mounted a probe or a mortar attack, Hale would discover he was gone. Yet Leander was always insubordinate to Hale, and done enough to receive a court martial from another commander.

Hale won't do a fucking thing, Jackson thought. Talk, that's all he'll do. Won't fuck with me because he'll be fucking with Light.

Breathing hard, Jackson began walking along the edge of the outermost circle of wire, hoping that someone on the perimeter would not open up on him. He tried to remember the ambush and listening post positions he had helped plot in grease pencil on the big map in the TOC. If he walked over one of them, they would kill him.

What about H&I fire, asshole? he thought. Harassment and Interdiction fire would be fired all night at random locations out in the bush.

Then the fear took hold of him so strongly that his legs failed him, and he had to sit down for a few minutes and take slow, deep breaths to calm himself.

Tom Light'll keep me from getting blown away, he thought over and over.

He walked on, carrying his M-16 on his hip with the safety off and his finger on the trigger, thinking that he did not want to be captured, remembering all the stories he had heard about what happened to American prisoners.

"Don't get captured," a cadre during basic training had told him. "They'll cut your ears and nose off and show'em to you while you're still alive. Use you for bayonet practice. They're not human."

Off to his right he saw the tall, dark shape of the tower as he walked through the scrub that covered the stretch of cleared ground toward the dark mass of forest. Sounds came out of it: buzzes and clicks and whistles made by the night animals.

Every time he stumbled over a vine or listened to a dry stick crack beneath his boots, he expected to see muzzle flashes from the enemy's weapons. And every bush and every small tree and every clump of grass looked like an enemy soldier crouched and ready to fire. But worst of all, after he stared at the dark shapes for a few seconds, they began to move. All around him the night was walking.

As he entered the trees it was much darker, and he felt safer. He crawled into a bamboo thicket and lay on the soft mat of leaves. Mosquitoes buzzed around his head and began to settle on his face despite the insect repellent he had rubbed on himself.

Jackson turned on the radio and pressed the transmission bar on the handset.

"Tom Light, Tom Light," he spoke in a whisper.

There was no reply, only static.

Just as he started to call again, he thought he saw something move in front of him. No bush this time. The M-16 lay on the leaves by his right knee.

Jackson began to choke for air, feeling so weak that he doubted if there would be strength in his arms to lift the rifle.

Whatever it was had stopped, a dark shape through the trees only a few meters away that looked to him like a crouching NVA. He looked to one side of it like he had been trained to do to see if it would go away, but it remained there, a black spot in the darkness.

Goddamn you, Tom Light, where are you? Jackson thought.

It moved again, and Jackson reached for the rifle. Then it ran, the brush crackling, and as he brought up the rifle he realized that it was one of those tiny deer, hardly bigger than a rabbit, that inhabited the forest. Every morning they came up to feed on the grass inside the wire. He sat down on the leaves shaking, soaked in sweat.

"Tom Light, Tom Light," Jackson whispered in the handset.

White noise was his reply.

Where was the rock? Jackson thought.

From the tower, getting to the rock looked easy, the outcropping a prominent feature of the ridge. Now he was uncertain how to find the rock, and the gunners at Desolation Row had begun to fire H&I fire, the rounds impacting perhaps a hundred meters away.

Suddenly Jackson felt the hand on his shoulder, and he wanted to reach for his rifle but could not. He was too scared to scream or even move. As he sucked in his breath to try to yell, a hand was placed over his mouth, and he felt hot breath on his ear.

"It's Tom," a voice said. "Hush up."

Jackson collapsed on the leaves, gasping for air, looking at the dark figure of Light who knelt above him, smelling the sharp scent of decaying leaves which was the stink of Light. There was a difference between Light's stink and the jungle smell of decay. Light's had something almost sweet to it, and Jackson supposed that the smell came from Light's rotting skin.

"Did you bring my letters?" Light asked, bending down to whisper to him.

Jackson still could not speak but nodded his head.

"I'll carry you to the rock. Next time I won't have to come get you," Light said.

By this time Jackson had calmed down enough to walk, so he got up and followed Light through the forest. Jackson kept getting tangled up in vines, most of which seemed to have thorns, but Light moved through the forest like he was walking along a road. Then in a clump of bamboo they were caught by H&I fire, the mortar rounds passing low over their heads. Jackson raised his head a little and watched the high explosive shells hit. The shell fragments glowed red in the dark, sailing toward them and cutting down sections of bamboo above their heads. He noticed he was breathing easily, his body feeling relaxed. Suddenly he felt Light's hand on the back of his neck, and his face was pushed down hard into the leaves.

"Keep down," Light said. "You'll get your fool head blowed off."

For the first time Jackson was enjoying the war in the way that his father had always claimed he had enjoyed his duty as an infantryman. Now with Light's protection he would go home with stories to tell around the fire at deer camp after the guns had been cleaned and racked, he sitting and drinking whiskey with the rest of the men.

Finally they walked up a narrow trail to the big rock, which was really not one rock but a series of rocky outcroppings on which little vegetation grew. The outcroppings ended in a cliff covered with vines and small trees, and Jackson saw the only way in or out was along the trail.

"What if they catch us here?" Jackson asked.

"There's another trail round the side of the cliff," Light said. "They won't come up here."

On the ridge below, Jackson saw flashes and heard the sound of enemy mortars firing. In a few seconds he saw the flashes at the firebase and heard the sound of the explosions. The mortar squad sent up illumination followed by high explosive rounds.

I'm fucked, Jackson thought.

Hale was up by now and mad as hell.

Well, just fuck it, Jackson thought. What could Hale do? Send me to Vietnam?

In the glow of the illumination, the small parachutes drifting over the rock, Jackson read Light his mail. Light's mother was doing better, and his father had been making good catches of fish. The old man was thinking about buying a new boat. Then Jackson wrote another letter for Light which was almost exactly like the first one.

The illumination was up and the guns still firing, but Jackson felt calm, breathing as easily as if he were sitting on the porch swing at home after supper.

Another series of mortar rounds were fired at the firebase from another location giving the firebase's mortars a new target.

"Our guns never kill any dinks. Blow up bamboo, that's all. Dinks up and gone by the time them rounds hit. Ain't I done for you like I promised? You'll get home," Light said.

"You're the fucking best," Jackson said.

"What're you going to do when you get home?" Light asked.

"Maybe go to college on the GI Bill. And you?"

"Fish. Nothing like going out and finding the lines full. A few channel cats run thirty or forty pounds. Cut some good catfish steaks off 'em."

More illumination went up and drifted over them.

Light continued, "But sometimes I don't know if I'd like to go home. I went home once. Couldn't get comfortable until I was back in country. Here's where I belong. Me and the starlight."

Jackson felt a tightness in his chest, hoping that Light was not going to start talking about seeing things in the starlight again.

"Home's where I want to be," Jackson said.

Light laughed and said, "Your time's just started. Later won't be so easy."

I won't end up like you, Jackson thought to himself. The day I get home I'll forget all about the war.

A gunship had been called in, and Jackson heard the grind of its Gatling guns, turning to watch the red tracers come down in an unbroken stream.

"I think the dinks have brought in a man," Light said.

"What man?" Jackson said.

"Someone like me, a sniper. I heard about him. They call him the Tiger. About three or four days ago he took a shot at me. Bullet hit a vine. Was a good shot. Never come up against a man before that could shoot like that," Light said.

What if Light was killed, Jackson thought. Then the sniper, better than Light, would kill all of them.

"Don't worry, I'll waste him," Light continued.

"Sure, you'll waste him," Jackson said.

It made sense. Light had never even been wounded. No one could stand against him.

"Have you got a girl?" Light asked.

"Yeah, she works in Birmingham," Jackson said.

"Does she write you?"

"Pretty often."

"Have you told her about me? How I'm going to keep you safe?"

"Yeah," Jackson said, wondering if somehow Light would know that he was lying.

"You'll go home and marry her and have kids?"

"Yeah. But there's lots of guys in Birmingham."

"Plenty of Jodys back in the world."

"Sure," Jackson said. Then he continued, "I've got to go back."

"Shit, wait till daylight."

"Hale ordered me not to go out. He was asleep when I left. He's up now and looking for me. I'm supposed to stay close to him with the radio."

"Let that bastard come out here if he wants the radio. He gives you any shit, you tell him I'll start living at the firebase. He can't stop me."

Nobody could fuck with Light. Nobody, Jackson thought.

Jackson and Light sat at the big rock and talked of home until morning. By then Jackson had learned all the details about Light's mother's bad heart, the commercial fishing business, his sister Ellen who lived in Memphis. He told Light about the farm and how much trouble it was to raise chickens, how on especially hot summer days you had to walk them in the chicken houses, keep them moving, or they would die of suffocation. Cleaning up used cars and selling them in Chicago was what interested Light most.

"That's smart," Light said. "I could learn to do that."

In the morning just before sunrise Light led him back through the jungle and left him at the edge of the scrub.

"Don't let Hale fuck with you," Light said.

"Keep my ass from getting blowed away," Jackson said.

"I never saw a man more worried about dying."

"I wrote your letters. Remember that."

"You keep listening on the radio. I'll call. You come out."

Then Light stepped away, disappearing into the jungle.

Jackson came out of the trees just as the sun rose over the mountains. All over the scrub were the small, white parachutes from the flares so that Jackson, basking in the warmth of the morning sun after the cool highland night, fancied that he was walking among the blossoms of gigantic white flowers.

When he reached the TOC, Hale was waiting.

"Pack up your shit. You're going to the fence," Hale said.

"Light won't like that," Jackson said.

"Goddamn, I don't care what he likes!" Hale shouted. "You're going to the fence."

Jackson gasped for breath and said, "You fuck with me, you fuck with Light. He'll come in. Stay here."

"See these!" Hale screamed, holding up his collar where his oak leaves were sewn in black thread. Then, talking fast, "No goddamn sniper is going to fuck with me. Don't even wear a uniform. Runs around in fucking dink sandals. Fucking starlight scope. Fucking rifle. I'm in command!''

Hale noticed that two lieutenants and a sergeant were standing in the corridor which led to the stairs. They looked like they were trying to decide whether to come in or go out. The radio operator at the big radio had become very interested in his log.

"What the fuck do you want?" Hale said. "Get out of there and kill the enemy."

The officers left.

Then Hale turned to Jackson and said, "You stay here. You go AWOL again and I'll ship your ass out to Hanoi."

Hale went into his cubicle, slamming the only door on the fire-base behind him, brought from the air-conditioned office Hale once had in Pleiku.

Jackson lay down on his cot, breathing hard.

I can go live out in the bush if I want, he thought. No more "fish on the bank." Light's going to make fucking sure nothing happens to me.

CHAPTER

7

THE NVA MADE IT HOT at the fence. The engineers measured their progress in meters. An enlisted man might dump a bag of concrete in a mixer and then spend the next hour flat on his back while the infantry tried to flush out a sniper. After weeks of work, only fifty meters of wire had been strung, most of that filled with holes from attacks by sappers.

Hale spent the time screaming over the radio at his platoon leaders down in the Cunt. Jackson was beginning to fear that Hale was going to go down and direct operations personally. Hale often cursed Light for not living up to his reputation as a killer of NVA.

It had just turned dark, and there was a firefight in progress in the Cunt.

"Goddamn, I don't care if you're understrength!" Hale shouted into the radio. "Keep them off the fence!"

Hale slammed down the handset.

Jackson noticed a soldier had come into the TOC. The man walked over to Hale.

"Major, I wanna join up with you," the soldier said.

"What's your name and unit, soldier?" Hale asked.

The soldier drew himself up straight, almost coming to attention, and said, "Private Savitch, Sir, Twenty-fifth Engineers."

"You're AWOL," Hale said.

"I'm not going back," Savitch said.

Jackson thought Hale would explode, but instead the major laughed.

Hale said, "No one volunteers for the infantry."

"I'm volunteering," Savitch said.

"Two Corps sends me replacements," Hale said. "Why should I take you?"

"I'm better at killing than stringing wire," Savitch replied.

"I should send you down to take the place of that goddamn sorry reserve lieutenant. He don't like it here at all. He wants to be back in his fraternity house," Hale said.

Savitch laughed and said, "I'm no college boy."

Hale had Jackson raise Little Tit on the radio, and after Hale promised the engineer CO two engineer replacements, the CO agreed to let Savitch stay. Hale told Savitch he could sleep that night in the TOC and in the morning he would assign him to one of the platoons. Then the major left.

Jackson learned Savitch was from Chicago and, like Jackson, had been drafted after high school. He had already been in country six months.

"Lemme tell you why I got away from the motherfucking engineers," Savitch said. "When I get in country they assign us to paving this road out of Bong Son over on the coast. Charlie don't like paved road. Can't mine it. First morning we go out Charlie hits the lead and rear trucks with B-40s, so our ass is stuck right there. By the time the gunships show up, me, O'Brien, and Washington are the only ones left alive out of the new guys. O'Brien got himself killed at the fence last week. Washington wasn't good for nothing after the ambush. They sent him home. That fence is worse than a hundred fucking Bong Sons. All those motherfucking engineers is gonna die."

"Tom Light'll kill the dinks," Jackson said.

"Yeah, I heard about that motherfucker. He's not so good. The dinks have been kicking ass," Savitch said.

"You wait, you'll see."

"I don't believe those stories. Yeah, he's greased a few dinks. He's not that good. Nobody is. Harry is as good as Light. Maybe better."

Then Savitch told him about an Australian mercenary named Harry.

"They were paying him $100 a man, $500 for officers," Savitch said. "After I finish my tour, I'm going into business for myself just like Harry. He gave me his address in Sydney. He'll show me the ropes, but he said I gotta have experience. If I don't get me some experience, I'll have to go back to Chicago. What's for me in Chicago? Nothing. Steal cars, maybe knock off a liquor store. I'll end up in Cook County Jail. All my friends are there. I can't be a fucking mercenary if I spend the war working on roads and fences. Men like Harry and Light can name their own price when the war's over."

"I want to go home," Jackson said.

"I'm not going home to work in a gas station."

"My cousin Leland does. What's wrong with that?"

"Not a thing, if you want to watch other people driving the big cars and getting the good-looking broads. Getting it whenever they want it. Everyone is making money out of this war but me. The chopper pilots are shooting tigers out of their ships and selling the skins in Hong Kong. They got a piece of the action in some whorehouse in Vung Tau. They'll go home rich."

"I'd pump gas the rest of my life if I could get out of here right now."

Savitch laughed and said, "Are you a farm boy, Jackson?"

"We run a few cows and some chickens. Only eighty acres. My daddy works at the steel plant in Birmingham," Jackson replied.

"You come to Chicago after the war. One week with me and you won't want to go back to the farm," Savitch said.

Jackson liked Savitch because the man was not afraid. Jackson wished that he could be like Savitch, go through the war without being afraid all the time.

"Don't you worry about getting blown away?" Jackson asked.

"Naw, I don't think about it. Sure, it could happen. Harry told me he liked it out in the bush. Things make sense out there. Did Tom Light tell you he was afraid?''

"No."

"I heard you spent the night in the bunker with him."

"Yeah."

"What did you talk about?"

"He doesn't talk much."

"Light's good. Harry's good. But I'm going to be better. Tell me one thing Light said."

"He said to keep my head down."

Savitch laughed and said, "Jackson, if you stayed here a hundred years you'd always be a fucking new guy."

The rest of the night Savitch talked of the money he was going to make as a mercenary and the broads, cars, and boats he was planning to buy with it.

In the morning Hale assigned Savitch to one of the platoons. After a few days, Jackson learned from Hale that Savitch had repeatedly volunteered for point.

"They can't kill Savitch," Hale said to Jackson one night. "Goddamn Light is probably dead. That son of a bitch Savitch smelled out an ambush yesterday. Lieutenant Hightower's platoon got three kills, the first ones that goddamn reserve lieutenant has made. You know what Savitch did? Put a bayonet on his rifle and practiced sticking dink corpses. Said he wanted to make sure his bayonet worked."

Hale laughed, and Jackson felt his stomach tighten.

"Morton can have Light back whenever he wants him. I got my own killer," Hale continued.

And then Savitch graduated from point man to infantry scout. One night in the TOC, Jackson watched Hale show Savitch a spot on the map where the Cunt narrowed into the gorge.

"There," Hale said jabbing his finger down on the map. "I think they're building bunkers somewhere up in these grid squares. Find them. We'll call in a B-52 strike."

"No problem, Major," Savitch, now a corporal, said.

Soon after Savitch rappelled down out of a helicopter into the jungle one night, the daylight attacks on the fence stopped. But the enemy still blew up sections of the fence in the early morning hours.

"See, he's reconning and killing at the same time," Jackson overheard Hale tell the first sergeant. "He's got the enemy on the run. He's already done more for us than that goddamn Light ever did."

Hale had Jackson try to contact Savitch on his walkie-talkie but with no success. Jackson decided that Savitch was either dead or had thrown the walkie-talkie away. The major insisted that Jackson log in ten attempts every day to contact his scout.

Another week passed and still the NVA left the fence alone during daylight. Jackson was asleep in the TOC one morning when he heard Hale calling his name. He opened his eyes and saw Hale standing over him.

"Get your radio and rifle," Hale said. "We're going to the fence."

As Jackson tied his boot laces, he watched the major putting on his steel pot and flak jacket. He guessed that the enemy had decided to make a daylight assault on the fence, and it had gotten so bad Hale had been forced to direct the defense personally. But nothing was coming over the big radio, the bored operator sitting by the machine drinking a cup of coffee.

Down at the fence Jackson got out of the chopper breathing hard. Gunships were circling overhead to provide security for the major. They followed the lieutenant in command of the platoon across the cleared ground which had grown up in scrub. A group of men were standing by the fence.

"Still haven't got it figured out, Major," a staff sergeant said.

Jackson saw there were men posted out in the scrub, their eyes fixed on the jungle. They followed the sergeant along the fence, and then Jackson saw the thing up on the fence post. Jackson gasped for breath, the hot, humid air feeling like water entering his lungs.

"They got it booby trapped," the sergeant continued. "We found one of the trip wires. My EOD man thinks they meant us to find it."

It was Savitch's head.

They all watched the emergency ordnance demolition man looking at the wire below the head.

Hale said, "I want that thing down."

"Yes, sir, he's the best," the sergeant said, nodding toward the EOD man. "He'll figure it out."

The EOD man backed carefully away from the wire and walked over the the sergeant. He and the sergeant talked to each other in low tones.

"Major, he thinks they've booby trapped the head," the sergeant said.

Jackson wished that the sergeant had not called it a head.

"I want it off the pole," Hale said.

Jackson could tell that Hale was getting mad, and the sergeant and the EOD man knew it too.

The sergeant and the EOD man walked off a little distance from the major and had another conference.

"Sir, he thinks the best thing to do is drop a frag on it," the sergeant said.

"Go ahead," Hale said.

Everyone took cover and the EOD man threw a frag out beside the post. The frag went off followed by an even louder explosion. Dirt fell down on top of Jackson who lay with his face pressed to the red clay. When the smoke and dust cleared, no head was on top of the pole.

"Jesus, they packed that thing full of TNT," the EOD man said.

Hale had the men search the scrub for remains but all that turned up were a few pieces of skin and a bit of skull with the hair still attached to it. No one at the fence had much to say. Jackson knew everyone was thinking of what their head would look like up on the pole.

As the chopper lifted off to take them back to the firebase, Jackson found he could breathe easy again. As it climbed over the Cunt, Jackson looked past the door gunner toward the gorge, thinking Light was somewhere in that sea of green and that the enemy would never put Light's head up on a pole.

CHAPTER

8

JACKSON WATCHED MAJOR HALE WORK at the map tripod beneath the bunker's single naked bulb. The TOC was the only bunker in camp with electricity. Sometimes the bulb burned very bright, but most of the time it was dim, illuminating only the center of the TOC and leaving the rest of the square room, especially the corners, in shadow. Hale was bent over the map on the table with a pencil in his hand. Occasionally he made a mark on the map with the pencil and then stared off into one of the dark corners. Jackson hoped Hale was not planning an attack on Holiday Inn base camp.

A conversation had just come over the radio between a company commander at Dak To and the medevac at Pleiku air base. The captain pleaded for a dust off, saying that many of his men, wounded in an attack which had just been beaten off, were going to die if they did not send a chopper. Jackson listened to the professionally calm voice from Pleiku tell the captain that they had none to send, and he would have to wait.

"These men are going to die!" the captain said. "Jesus, send me something!"

Then the transmission was broken off abruptly, but the captain

55

must have held down the transmission bar for a second because Jackson heard the sound of small-arms fire and men yelling. Hale, still lost in thought, had paid no attention to the conversation.

The radio was silent, and the operator dialed another frequency out of Dak To. As the operator twisted the dial, Jackson noticed a strange smell in the bunker. Hale smelled it too, for he looked up from his maps, both men at the same time seeing the figure standing in the semidarkness at the doorway of the bunker, which was even darker than the corners because it was at the end of a narrow hallway. It was that rotting leaf smell but with something added that Jackson could not identify.

Tom Light stepped out of the darkness, crossing the room to Hale. Jackson wondered why Light had not called him on the radio again to tell him he was coming in.

"I told you not to come back without confirmation," Hale said.

"I know," Light said.

Hale said, "How in hell did you get back in here? The front gate has orders not to let you inside the wire."

Hale rang up front gate on the field telephone.

"I didn't come in the gate," Light said.

Hale stood there looking at Light with the phone in his hand.

"No chopper has landed. How?" Hale asked.

"I'm here," Light said. "It don't matter how."

Hale put the phone down.

"Does anyone know you're here?" Hale asked.

"No," the sniper said, reaching into his pocket and taking out something wrapped in fresh leaves.

The leaves, Jackson thought, must have been the reason for the unusual smell. Light was unwrapping the leaves, and Jackson moved closer. Then Light had it in his hand and Hale, recoiling, stepped back, the stench filling the bunker. Light dropped it on the map, the severed cock landing with a splat, the black clotted blood dribbling a trail across the white paper. Jackson thought of the black rubber snakes he bought when he was a boy and hid under the sheets of his sister's bed. If left on a window sill, the snakes would turn soft and melt in the sun, losing their round shape, flattening out. That was what it looked like.

The cutting had been done with a razor sharp knife, no rough edges left where it had been lopped off. Jackson, gasping for air, did not want to look at it, wished that the generator would suddenly fail, plunging the bunker into darkness, and when the bulb glowed again Light and the thing on the map table would be gone. Although trying hard to stay cool, Hale had taken another step back from the table.

The thing had obviously been taken several days before, since it had turned a dark brown from its original yellow and had shrunk to the size of an infant's. It was uncircumcised. Jackson wondered if all of them were like that. The smell of the thing was something he knew he would always remember.

Hale finally spoke, his voice shrill and uneven, "Get that thing off my table!"

"I want my R&R," Light said, making no move toward the table.

"That's just one," Hale said. "I want you back out in the bush."

Light took off his floppy bush hat and pulled his dogtag chain over his head. He threw it on the table. Jackson saw in the place of dogtags there was something strung on the chain looking like pieces of dried fruit. He realized that the sniper had taken his trophies and dried them in the sun, afterwards stringing them on the chain.

"Count'em," Light said. "There's six. I took the fresh one on the ridge west of your camp three days ago. He was down in a spider hole. You need a recon, Major. There're beaucoup NVA up there. One of these nights they're gonna come down here and cut off yours."

"I want goddamn bodies," Hale said.

Light smiled and said, "You know, Major, once I had a company commander made us count smells. We'd shelled a bunker complex. Bodies buried under dirt and logs. So he made us sniff at the holes and cracks. Like a pack of rabbit dogs nosing a brush pile. We turned in them smells. Probably got himself a promotion out of it."

"Bodies," Hale said.

"Once these are dried in the sun they turn black as the inside of your asshole," Light said. "No difference between a round eye and a gook dick. Americans'd be lot easier to kill than the dinks."

The bulb began to fade, leaving Hale outside the circle of light. But Jackson could still see Light clearly. He was looking toward Hale, waiting for an answer. Hale was mad but was trying hard to control himself.

"In the morning," Hale said. "There's not a chopper available."

Jackson took some slow, deep breaths as he thought of the NVA massing up on the ridge. Light would not be around to protect him.

"Then get one from Pleiku," Light said.

"It's a hot night," Hale said. "The NVA are pushing hard up at Dak To."

"Now," Light said.

The bulb glowed bright again, so bright that Jackson wondered if it would explode from the sudden surge of power coming from the generator. Hale looked like he wished it would, so he would be protected from Tom Light by the darkness. In the glare Jackson saw every crease in the major's face, the network of wrinkles around his eyes. Hale looked old, making Jackson think of his grandfather.

"You'll have your chopper and your R&R, but I want you back here in three goddamn days," Hale said. "Don't plan to set foot in this camp."

Light grinned and said, "There's plenty NVA in the mountains. I'll be back."

"Get me General Morton's headquarters. Put it on the secure net," Hale said to Jackson.

Once Jackson had raised the general's headquarters, he placed the transmission on a scrambler so that neither the Americans nor the enemy could eavesdrop on the conversation. Hale took over the radio and asked to speak to the general.

"Light's here in my TOC, Sir," Hale said. "He's got his kills and wants to chopper out of here for R&R. My ships are gone. If the men find out he's here, I could have a mutiny on my hands. I need a chopper for him now."

"He can wait," the general's voice came over the speaker.

Hale said, "General, you sent him up here. I can't protect the fence if my men mutiny."

The general paused and said, "Goddamn it, Hale, you better not have a mutiny up there, or I'll have your head. I sent him because he kills the enemy. He's got more kills than your entire battalion. The fence is behind schedule. Those engineers haven't strung enough wire to fence my backyard. If you'd do more killing and less worrying about Light, we'd have it built. He'll have his chopper. Don't call me again for something like this. Out."

"You stay down here until the chopper comes," Hale said to Light. "Jackson, get rid of those things."

"Where?" Jackson asked.

"Burn, bury, throw'em out in the wire," Hale said. "Take that map too."

Light went over to one of the dark corners and after propping the rifle up against the side of the wall squatted gook fashion.

Jackson stood by the map tripod and looked at Light's trophies. He was not sure if he was going to be able to touch them.

"Leave the chain," Light said.

Jackson unsnapped the chain and pushed the dried cocks off it. They had dried to the consistency of leather and did not smell, having lost almost all resemblance to what they once were. The fresh one was another matter. He did not want to touch it, so he wrapped it up in Hale's map of Laos. Going out of the TOC, he went down by the latrine and with an entrenching tool dug a hole and buried them.

Back at the TOC he found Hale busy with his maps again and Light still squatting in the corner. Hale left the TOC, leaving Jackson alone with Light. Jackson sat at the radio and waited for Light to speak to him.

"The major wanted proof," Light said.

Jackson turned to face the dark shape that was Light.

"You could've radioed."

"Look, they were dead when I done it to'em. A dick's the only thing a man has got one of besides a nose that's easy to take and carry. I met an Australian mercenary out there once who took noses. Thought I'd do something different.''

Jackson said nothing.

"They do worse than I've done," Light said. "You can't hurt the dead. That general the major was talking to sent some LRRP patrol up in those mountains around that big base camp. I made contact with'em. Told'em the dinks knew exactly where they was right from the time they rappelled down into the big trees out of the chopper. That goddamn lieutenant didn't listen to a fucking thing I said. Next time I saw him was in the forest about a day after the dinks had ambushed'em. Every man had his dick cut off and stuffed in his mouth. The lieutenant chewed his half in two. So I know they'd did it to him while he was still alive. Trying to spit it out to breathe, I guess.''

"I don't want to kill anyone. I couldn't mutilate bodies," Jackson said.

"You're no better than me, base camp soldier. We're all here to kill the dinks.''

"You like it.''

"No, it's just what I do.''

"You could live out in the bush until your tour is over.''

"They'd leave me out in the bush until the old Mississippi dried up unless I kill. Until all those troops started dying when they went out with me, I was like you. Waiting to go home. Counting the days. Then all those troops got wasted. Decided this fucking place was where I belonged. You belong here too. Just don't know it yet.''

"I don't belong here.''

Light laughed softly. "You got a long ways to go before you climb on that freedom bird.''

Light paused and sighed before he continued, "Maybe one day I'll just quit. It ain't the dinks or the bugs or the jungle rot or eating snakes and lizards. It's being alone. Sometimes it's like there's nobody left in the world but me.''

Light's talk about being lonely made Jackson uneasy. That made Light an ordinary man, not someone who could keep him alive.

"You got to come on R&R with me," Light said.

"Hale won't let me," Jackson said. "I've only been in country two months."

"You have to go. Hale's RTO is gonna die. I saw it in the scope." Jackson gasped for breath.

"Calm down," Light continued. "You're going with me."

"We need to tell Hale not to get another RTO. Warn him," Jackson said.

"Can't do nothing about it. It's in the scope. Done. Finished. You stay, you'll get wasted."

"You stay, keep me from getting blown away."

"Nothing I can do. I saw it in the scope. It's gonna happen."

Hale came back into the TOC.

"Jackson's going with me," Light said.

"He's not going anywhere," Hale said.

Jackson thought of walking up the long concrete walk to Loretta's house, she waiting on the porch, he trying hard to remember how she looked, her green eyes, red hair.

"Then I'll take my R&R right here," Light said. "I got three days this time instead of one night."

Hale said, "Goddamn, you think you can do any fucking thing you want. Got lucky and walked away from those ambushes. Lucky is all you are. Goddamn dinks are kicking our ass at the fence. I need Jackson. I need more troops."

"He goes, or I stay," Light said.

Hale paused before he spoke.

"Jackson, you're fucking crazy to go with him. Watch out or you'll end up like Light. No friends. Everyone scared shitless of you." And then he turned to Light. "I'm not afraid of you. You can die just like any other man. One of these days somebody'll put a round through your head."

"Plenty have tried," Light said.

"Don't set foot on this firebase again," Hale said. "I'm giving the perimeter instructions to fire on you."

Light laughed. "You're supposed to be fighting the dinks, not me."

"Get the fuck out of here!" Hale yelled.

Jackson followed Light up the steps. The chopper was waiting at the pad, and when it lifted off, Jackson wished he did not have to return to Desolation Row again. He saw Light sitting slumped in his seat, the rifle wrapped in the poncho.

What's in that fucking scope, Jackson thought.

Then he thought of Hale's new RTO and wondered who it was going to be. He hoped Hale picked a new man, someone Jackson did not know.

CHAPTER

9

AT VUNG TAU THEY CHECKED into a hotel. The town was on a plain between two mountains and looked out on the sea. They had both changed into new fatigues at Pleiku, and Jackson noticed Light kept his bush hat pulled down low over his eyes. Light now looked like an ordinary soldier, but even after a shower the jungle stink still remained on his body.

"Don't write down my name," Light said as Jackson started to sign the register.

So Jackson wrote only his own name but the Vietnamese clerk at the desk did not give them the key.

"You name please, Sir," the clerk said and smiled, offering the pen to Light.

Jackson took the pen and wrote, Melvin Hale.

The clerk looked at the signature and handed over the key.

"Welcome to Vung Tau, Mr. Hale," the clerk said to Light.

Light grinned.

"First we get something to eat," Light said. "Next we'll hit the beach. Then find some girls."

On a terrace at the USO they ate steak and drank cold beer. Across the street was a school, the yard filled with children at recess. Jackson noticed no one was carrying weapons except for security people, but Light still had his rifle wrapped up in a poncho. It leaned against one of the extra chairs. Jackson had learned from Light that Vung Tau was a kind of free zone. The VC left the town alone, seldom mounting any rocket or mortar attacks. Occasionally there was a kidnapping or an assassination.

When they had ridden in from the airfield on a bus with grenade screens over the windows, Jackson saw two-story houses painted in pastel colors. Light told him there were big villas outside of town, built by Saigon politicians and generals who were growing rich off the war. The larger houses in town all had walls built around them topped with bits of broken glass. Many had RPG screens and concertina wire attached to the tops of the walls. In the compounds roses grew, but they all looked withered and in need of water. Pepper and eucalyptus trees were planted in rows along the streets. The power poles were like those in an American town.

Jackson noticed a group of Vietnamese standing on the street and staring toward their table. One of them was an old man with a beard who led a little girl by the hand. When they saw Jackson looking at them, they smiled and walked away.

"What do those people want?" Jackson asked Light.

"Sell us something," Light said.

The old man and the little girl did not return.

When they left the USO Jackson felt good, a little drunk from the beer, his stomach full of steak. They took a bus to the beach.

At the beach Jackson and some other soldiers rented a ski boat. Light sat under an awning and drank beer. Jackson could almost imagine he was at Pensacola except for the fact there were soldiers in fatigues. A band was playing in a compound but there were no girls, the drunken soldiers dancing with each other.

Jackson skied all afternoon. Then he returned to the beach and sat with Light under the awning. Just as Jackson lay back on the sand to go to sleep, he saw the old man and the little girl. They stepped out from behind a stand that sold hamburgers, and the old man pushed her toward where he and Light were sitting. The little girl carried a Styrofoam cooler.

"Hey, GI. Want a beer?" she asked.

Jackson paid for his beer. Then the girl went over to Light who sat with his back against the tree, facing the town. But instead of giving Light his beer, she just stood and stared at him. Suddenly she ran off toward the town, leaving the cooler.

Light started to open it.

"Stop!" Jackson said, thinking the cooler might be booby trapped.

Light laughed and tilted the open cooler toward Jackson. It was filled with beer, not high explosives.

"Dinks are crazy," Light said.

Jackson finished his beer and lay in the sun. When he got hot, he went to the sea, wading out until he was waist-deep in the warm, clear water. Out off the cape a line of freighters moved past on their way to and from Saigon, seventy or eighty miles away. Jackson swam out from the beach and dove, spreading his arms out wide and floating, feeling his body relax, the war fading away. He wished he could stay under that warm water, not have to surface to breathe.

A Vietnamese fishing boat had moved in and dropped its nets just outside a bar. Small bail fish began to jump, pursued by a school of porpoise.

I could get them to take me out to a ship, Jackson thought.

Jackson floated on his back, letting the tide carry him. The beach looked far away, the sound of the music from the band growing faint. Then he saw a figure on the beach waving its arms.

Light. Wants me to come in, Jackson thought.

He turned from the open sea and swam back toward the beach.

They left the beach and took a bus into town. It was like walking through K-Mart, Jackson thought. Everywhere vendors had black-market American goods for sale: boxes of soap, shaving cream, soft drinks, beer, stereos, tape decks, watches.

"Hey, GI, you want boom-boom?" a boy no more than ten or twelve said to Light. "Numba one."

Light gave the boy money and they followed him down a side-street.

The boy stopped at a two-story house. They went in through a passageway and then up on the roof of the first story. Girls and soldiers were there. A group of soldiers who all wore thirty-eights in shoulder holsters were sitting around in bathrobes. Music came from speakers set on the rail of the terrace.

Light found a girl first. Jackson watched him walk off with her into the house, one arm around the girl and the other around the rifle.

Then Jackson followed him with a girl. She wore a T-shirt with the words "Playboy Bunny" on it. In the tiny room created by a plywood partition, open to the high ceiling at the top, she took off her clothes and lay down on a bed made of two mattresses stacked on the floor.

Jackson lowered himself into her, a tiny girl with big breasts, and tried to forget about Desolation Row. Then it was over quicker than he had expected. He gave her more money and waited for himself to be ready again. She brought him a beer.

There was a couple in the next cubicle. Their mattress creaked.

"Boom-boom," Jackson's girl said, and laughed.

"Starlight, starlight!" a girl's voice yelled.

"Leave that alone," Light said.

People were talking rapidly in Vietnamese out in the hall. Jackson pushed open the door. The old man and little girl from the beach stood in the hall. Beside them was a Vietnamese soldier dressed in tiger-stripe fatigues.

"Tom Light, Tom Light." the child screamed.

Light came out of his cubicle, the rifle in his hands. The little girl ran up to him and began to speak rapidly to Light in Vietnamese. Jackson could tell from the expression on Light's face that he understood none of it.

"My brother is dead. You come," the soldier said.

"Get the fuck away from me," Light said.

The soldier said, "He has only been dead one day. You come."

The little girl took hold of Light's sleeve and tugged at it, speaking to him in Vietnamese. Light turned and walked away, pushing half-dressed soldiers out of the way.

"You talk to Tom Light," the soldier said to Jackson. "My brother is dead."

The soldier began to cry, and the little girl began to chant Light's name.

"I don't know—" Jackson began. "I don't know any Tom Light." Jackson ran down the hall and out of the house. Light was waiting for him out on the street.

"Why'd you leave me?" Jackson asked.

"Goddamn crazy dinks. I didn't even get a chance with that girl. She got my money," Light said.

"What did they want?"

"Forget it. Just a bunch of crazy dinks. Let's get out of this fucking town."

As they walked to the hotel Jackson kept asking Light questions, but Light refused to talk.

"You go in. Get our shit," Light said.

"What's going on?" Jackson asked. "What did they want back there?"

"Goddamn dink at the desk recognized me," Light said. "I know it was him. We've got to get the fuck out of here before they find me. We're going back to the fucking bush."

"I'm not going fucking anywhere. What the fuck is going on!" Jackson said.

"Goddamn dinks. They believe the whole fucking country is full of witches and spirits. Think I can raise the fucking dead with the starlight."

Jackson took a deep breath and asked, "Can you?"

"Shit no. Are you fucking crazy? I see things in the starlight. Sometimes I know when a man's gonna die. Think I'd be in this fucking war if I could do that kind of shit?"

Jackson went into the hotel. The same clerk was at the desk. He smiled when Jackson came in. Jackson went up to the room and got their bags.

"We're checking out," Jackson told the clerk.

"Did you and Mr. Hale enjoy your stay?" the clerk asked.

"Sure, it was great," Jackson said.

He took a good look at the clerk and wondered if Light was right about him.

They caught a ride on a truck going to the airfield. Soon they were aboard a C-130 headed for Pleiku. Light almost immediately went to sleep in the jump seat beside Jackson, his hat pulled down over his eyes.

"Hey, man, you hear about Tom Light in Vung Tau?" the soldier sitting on the other side of Jackson said.

"No," Jackson said, hoping the soldier would shut up.

"Slopes found Tom Light at some whorehouse," the soldier said. "Fucking crazy slopes. Think that starlight scope of his can raise the dead. Wanted Light to raise a dead ARVN. Fucking ARVN probably died of fright. They never get close enough to the shit to get shot. Dinks get everything backwards. Light wastes slopes, he don't raise'em."

The soldier laughed and Jackson with him.

"Yeah, fucking crazy," Jackson said.

Jackson looked at Light who was snoring. He had always been afraid of Light, but now the fear was different. Light had struck something deep within him, that same sort of thing that set dogs howling at the moon.

He had experienced that kind of feeling one morning when he went hunting with Uncle Frank. Jackson noticed a crowd in front of the bait shop where they always ate breakfast. Running ahead he pushed his way through the crowd, reached the last row of men, and stumbled forward, hearing the buzzing noise at the the same time his face came to within a few inches of the wire cage. He saw the diamond pattern of it, the thing uncoiling faster than he could have imagined, his head ringing against the taut wire, the poison splattering in his face like a light rain. The men laughed.

Afterward Frank helped him wash off his face with a hose. He was till shaking and gasping for breath.

"Nothing to be scared about, just a snake in a cage," Frank said. "Worry about the ones in the woods."

Light had kept him alive. He was not a man Jackson should fear.

Yet there was that crazy business at Vung Tau. And Light telling the future by looking at the pictures in the scope. The plane began its combat descent into Pleiku, coming down at a sudden, steep angle. Jackson gasped for breath, but Light slept through it all.

CHAPTER

10

JACKSON AND LIGHT HITCHED a ride on a chopper to Desolation Row. Light was dressed in cut-off fatigues, a sweater, and dink sandals again. Instead of landing at the pad, the chopper touched down in the scrub outside the wire. Hale was making good on his threat never to let Light inside the wire again. Jackson thought that Light might protest, but instead he laughed and jumped out of the chopper. The door gunner covered him as Light waved goodbye and walked off through the scrub.

Jackson walked in to the TOC and found Hale at work on his maps. A sergeant and two lieutenants were with him. All the way back to Desolation Row, he had been wondering if he would find Hale's RTO alive or dead. He looked around the TOC for the man. The radio was on a cot. Maybe he had gone to the latrine.

"Sniper got him last night," Hale said.

Jackson sat down on a cot and took deep, slow breaths.

"He was a new man, a dud. Lit a cigarette without shielding it. Got him right between the eyes."

Hale and the officers laughed, but Jackson felt sick. Jackson was glad it was not him, but he had not wanted the man to die. Better for no one to die. But what appeared in the starlight was going to happen, no way to avoid it.

Later Hale went to sleep and Jackson took the radio and left the TOC. From a bunker near the four-deuce mortar pits, he heard music. He went into the bunker. Candles were set in empty C-rations cans. The mortar squad sat on shell boxes listening the the Rolling Stones on a battery-powered tape recorder, the bunker filled with smoke from the pipe they were passing around.

"Have a hit, man," a soldier said. "Little opium makes this grass taste sweet."

Jackson accepted the pipe and filled his lungs with smoke. He wanted to get high, to forget about Light.

"Ain't you Alabama, the dude that's friends with Light?" another soldier asked.

"I'm Hale's RTO," Jackson replied.

"But the major don't need no radio man," the same soldier said. "He don't go outside the wire."

All the men laughed.

Leander was there, still wearing his pith helmet.

"Hey, Leander, you think Alabama draws fire like Light?" a soldier said.

"Looks like he'd draw fire," Leander said.

Someone turned down the music.

Jackson decided to say nothing, wishing he had not smoked. Instead of feeling good, watching the colors and listening to the music slow down, the guitar runs almost frozen in time, he was beginning to feel uneasy. His chest grew tight, and he took a deep breath to try to relax.

Another soldier said in a slow, thick voice, "I bet this mo'fucker draws fire, just like Tom Light."

"That LRRP team in the Ia Drang Valley got themselves fucked because of him," the soldier who had offered him the hit said.

"Yeah, that's so," Leander said. "Ain't you Light's bro? Went on R&R with him. You go out to the graveyard with him and dig up dead dinks?"

Jackson said nothing. That was the same rumor he had heard in Pleiku at the airbase.

"We thought Dak To was the bad shit," another soldier said.

"Nothing worse than this crazy ass place. I get an R&R out of here, I'm not coming back. I'll volunteer for an LRRP team. Anything's better'n this."

"Fucker, don't you come messing around this bunker no more," Jackson heard Leander say to him, the man's voice pot cool, soft and calm. "Nothing personal. Don't want to go home in no sloppy rubber bag because of you."

No one took up his defense, and Jackson left the bunker, hearing the men laughing behind him.

Tom Light's got my ass covered, Jackson thought.

Jackson laughed softly to himself as he thought of what they might have done if they had known about Light's prediction. That might have been enough to set off the mutiny Hale worried about.

Now he was stoned and wished he could have stayed with the mortar squad and listened to music. He went to the TOC and climbed up the sandbags. The sandbags had recently been painted with tar to keep water out of the bunker, and the tar, still soft from the heat of the day, stuck to his hands and the seat of his fatigues. On the perimeter someone on a heavy machine gun began firing out into the bush. He listened to the slow chug of the gun and watched the red tracers, fascinated by the way they glowed. Like fireworks, he thought, the machine gun a giant Roman candle. The gun stopped, the gunners popped a flare.

And Jackson, stoned beyond fear, lay back on the sandbags and watched the magnesium flare crackle and sparkle, showers of white sparks dropping off as its parachute carried it over the wire.

Jackson turned on the radio.

"Tom Light, Tom Light," he spoke into the handset, as he had night after night after night, receiving no reply.

He began to wonder if he would ever see Light again. It was easy for him to imagine Light wandering off through the jungle, walking the ridges of the Long Mountains toward China.

No reply, only the white noise from the handset. Another flare went up on the perimeter and a gunner fired a long burst on an M-60 machine gun. He's going to burn up the barrel, Jackson thought. Perhaps there were sappers in the wire, but the response was not frantic enough for that. The firing stopped and more flares went up. He lay on his back, watching them sparkle.

Jackson picked up the handset again.

"Loretta, Loretta, Loretta," he said, releasing the handset's transmission bar.

And although he did not hear his girl's voice come out of the handset, and did not want to hear it because that would mean he was as crazy as Light, he imagined what she would say.

"Jackson, I'm waiting for you," her soft voice spoke within his head.

He tried to figure out whether it would be day or night back in the world. If it was day she would be at her typewriter in the lawyer's office in Birmingham, and if it was night she would be at her apartment which she shared with another girl.

"I'll meet you in Hawaii for R&R," Jackson said into the handset.

Static hissed from the handset. Jackson, even though stoned, knew he was imagining the whole conversation, but he had heard her voice. A little breeze came up, and he shivered. He buttoned the top button of his fatigue jacket.

"We'll stay in a hotel right on the beach," he said.

"All day in bed with you," she said.

A soldier walked past the TOC. Jackson wondered if the man had overheard him. Then Jackson imagined he was undressing her, feeling her warm, smooth skin against his fingers, fumbling with hooks and buttons. He worried about getting the tar on her which had stuck to his hands. Now he was hard, his dick tight against his fatigues. She was unbuttoning his fly.

"I'll send you money for a ticket," he said.

"I'm waiting for you," she said.

Jackson could see her clearly—breasts, legs, the dark patch of hair. He ran his hands over her body, explored with his fingertips between her thighs.

"I'm coming home," he said. "Nothing will stop me."

"Yes," she said.

Now her voice was clearly coming out of the handset, not out of his mind. Jackson sat shivering in the breeze, cold except for the hot place between his legs.

"Just for me, Loretta," he said.

"Yes."

And Jackson thought that it was not real because she was agreeing to everything. He wondered if she agreed with whatever the men in Birmingham suggested to her. There appeared a picture in his mind of her bent over one of them in bed, her mouth over his dick, just as large and erect as Jackson's was now. She could do as she liked, and there was absolutely nothing he could do to stop her. She could suck and fuck every man in Birmingham, dance in one of the topless bars, walk the streets, and there was nothing, nothing he could do.

"Loretta, you wouldn't—" he began.

"No, just for you," she whispered. "Just for you."

And the imaginary voice broke across the static and filled his ears coming out of the night, out of nothingness. Jackson looked up at the star-filled but still moonless sky and wished he could hide her away from all the Jodys in that blackness.

"Loretta, you promised me," he said.

"Tom Light, Tom Light!" a shrill dink voice came out of the handset.

Jackson lost his hardon in a instant, lying atop the bunker breathing heavily as if he had just spent himself in the girl.

"Tom Light, you motherfucker!" the high-pitched dink voice said again. "We kill you!"

Laughter from the handset.

"Light'll waste your dink ass!" Jackson said into the handset between gasps.

"Someone fucking you girlfriend right now," the dink voice said. "All at Desolation Row die. No one have a nice day."

Jackson wanted to switch the radio off but could not. He wondered if Light was listening, wished Light would come on the frequency and tell the slope his ass was as good as greased.

"Tom Light, Tom Light," Jackson said.

"The jungle is our friend," the dink voice said again. "The jungle has killed Tom Light."

"He's out there," Jackson said. "He'll blow you away."

More laughter. To stop it Jackson pressed down on the transmission bar and shouted, "Tom Light! Tom Light!"

But still there was nothing, only the hiss of static. Jackson switched the radio off and felt like crying. He wanted to smell the jungle smell of Tom Light, but instead there was the sharp, sour stink of a piss tube in the air.

The mortars began firing, and Jackson stood up to watch the impacts. When the rounds hit up on the ridge, a series of flashes, it was with the soft whump of willie peter instead of the sharp crack of high explosive. He lay back on the sandbags and imagined that white phosphorous cloud of fire dropping down on the dink he had just talked to on the radio. Now the night was quiet.

Jackson stretched out on the sandbags and tried to push the war out of his mind by concentrating on the beautiful vision of colors he had begun to see, hoping they would twist and flow into the shape of Loretta.

Suddenly without warning the fear took hold of him, sucking the air out of his lungs. He saw Tom Light walking through the jungle and a squad of NVA crouched in ambush on both sides of a trail preparing to catch Light in a crossfire from which there was no possibility of escape. Then the dinks sprang the ambush.

"Run! run!" he screamed, and he was in the forest too, running toward the sound of the firing, his feet becoming tangled in vines, running and falling, running and falling.

He reached the ambush, but there was no more firing. Tom Light stood on the trail with a smile on his face, the rifle with the starlight scope in his hands.

"You ain't never gonna be short," Light said.

"Loretta! Loretta!" Jackson shouted, suddenly feeling the sticky tar of the sandbags beneath his hands instead of the wet litter of the jungle floor.

CHAPTER

11

THE REPLACEMENT FINALLY ARRIVED for the communications specialist killed while serving as Hale's RTO.

"There's a new radio operator coming in today," Hale said. "Name's Labouf. What kind of goddamn name is that?"

"Don't know, sir," Jackson replied.

"You meet him at the pad. Help him get squared away. Don't get him fucking around with Light, Jackson."

"Yes sir," Jackson said.

Jackson went to the pad and found a soldier sitting on a footlocker which had chain wrapped around it secured with padlocks.

"Labouf?" Jackson asked.

"Yo," the dark-skinned man said and grinned. "We're all going to die up here, right?"

Labouf was a short man with curly black hair. Maybe a Greek.

"It's not that bad," Jackson said.

Jackson liked playing the role of a veteran. But he noticed Labouf's uniform was not new.

"That's not what I heard. If it wasn't bad, I wouldn't be here," Labouf said.

He knelt down and began examining the footlocker, running his fingers along a small crack along one side.

"Those dickheads threw it out of the chopper," he complained. "Didn't even give me a chance to help them with it. Fucked it up."

Jackson had never seen a replacement arrive with a footlocker before. Soldiers in Saigon or one of the big base camps had footlockers but not at Desolation Row.

"What you got in there?" Jackson asked.

Labouf smiled. "Personal stuff. The army lets you keep personal stuff in a footlocker," he replied.

Labouf lifted the footlocker to his shoulder. Whatever was in it was not that heavy and did not make noise.

"Where's the radio?" Labouf asked.

Jackson led him to the TOC where they found Major Hale working at his map tripod.

"What the hell have you got in that footlocker, soldier?" Hale asked.

"Personal stuff, Sir," Labouf said. "Like to keep it down here."

"Go ahead," Hale said. "Jackson here is buddies with Tom Light. Those that hang around with Light get blown away."

"He's still alive. Must be lucky," Labouf said.

Jackson liked the sound of that. Someone considered him lucky.

"No one's lucky enough to get close to Light," Hale said and left the TOC.

Labouf shoved his footlocker under a cot. Jackson learned Labouf was a first-generation American whose family was from Lebanon and now lived in Philadelphia. He had been drafted and sent to Vietnam where he had gotten into some sort of difficulty while working in Saigon at American headquarters.

"Hey, I got some good stuff," Labouf said. "Want to smoke."

"Sure," Jackson said.

The found an empty bunker. Labouf had cigarettes, the tobacco taken out and replaced with marijuana, the ends twisted to hold it in.

Jackson filled his lungs with smoke. Soon he was feeling good. He saw Labouf smiling at him.

"I'm going home rich," Labouf said. "You want to make some money?"

Jackson remembered Savitch.

"You running drugs back to the States?"

"Shit, no. Too risky. I had a buddy. The fucking FBI delivered his stuff to his house after he went home. They got dogs sniffing every package, all the hold baggage. I ain't stupid." Labouf continued, "I was playing the black market money game, doubling my paycheck every month and then doubling that. The CID got on to me, but I made a deal with them, put the finger on the guys that's really cleaning up. They promised I was going home. Next thing I know I get orders to come up here. They're trying to kill me. Nobody's going to be killing Ernest Labouf. All I had time to do was grab my stash. No chance to get it home. Couldn't walk into the Bank of America and deposit fifty thousand dollars. The CID guys were probably waiting for me."

Why was Labouf telling him what was in the locker, Jackson thought.

"I heard about Tom Light," Labouf said. "No one is going to fuck with his friends. This locker will be safe in here. Help me guard it. Keep your mouth shut. You can have a cut for your trouble, a couple of thousand. We'll smuggle this out in our baggage when we go home. Maybe I can get back to Saigon. I got this contact at the Bank of America who maybe can get it out of the country for us. But not right now. Too hot to risk it."

"Hale will never let us go to Saigon," Jackson said.

"I'll think of a way," Labouf said. "I don't want to get blown away fucking around with Light."

"Don't worry about Light. He's covering my ass," Jackson said.

"What can he do for you from out in the bush?"

"I go out there. With him," Jackson said.

Labouf laughed and said, "I'm not going out." He paused before he continued, "Any asshole fucks with this footlocker I'll kill'em."

"The guard at the TOC won't let an enlisted man near the entrance," Jackson said. "Hale's afraid of getting fragged."

"They sure better not fuck with my footlocker," Labouf said.

After that, Jackson occasionally wondered if Labouf was lying and considered prying open the locker to have a look. But he was afraid it might be booby trapped, and he believed Labouf's threat.

Then Jackson noticed Reynolds & Raymond began to shadow Labouf. Jackson stood at the entrance to the TOC and watched Labouf walk across the compound. Reynolds walked in front, playing his M-16, and Raymond behind. They reached the TOC and Labouf turned on Raymond.

"Keep the fuck away from me," Labouf said.

Reynolds sang, "Take anything you want from me, anything/Fly on little wing."

"Hey, money man, we're watching out after you," Raymond said.

"Quit calling me that," Labouf said.

"It's the truth ain't it. Ain't you the money man. Got his footlocker filled with money."

Reynolds giggled.

"You better not be out here when I get off duty," Labouf said.

Reynolds put his M-16 behind his head and played it.

"You hear me," Labouf continued. "Keep the fuck away."

Jackson followed Labouf into the TOC.

"What do those two fuckers want?" Labouf asked. "You didn't tell'em about my money?"

"Hell, no. Those two are so fucked up on speed they'll never come down. When they do, the crash'll sound like an arclight," Jackson said.

Labouf continued to threaten them, but Reynolds & Raymond paid no attention to him. Wherever Labouf went in the camp, Reynolds & Raymond were with him, one walking in front and one behind.

Jackson had gone to sleep on the cot when he heard something rattling. He opened his eyes and saw Reynolds & Raymond sitting on Labouf's footlocker. Labouf was not at the big radio or on his cot. The radio operator on duty sat with his feet up on the table and his bush hat pulled down over his eyes. Asleep.

"Where's Labouf?" Jackson asked.

"Gone," Raymond said.

Reynolds played with the chain on the locker and examined one of the locks. Jackson wondered if he could pick it.

"How did you get in here?" Jackson asked.

"Guard's stoned," Raymond said. "Raymond played him a little 'Purple Haze,' on his 'sixteen and he said drive on."

Jackson said, "Hale'll be down here anytime."

"Up in the tower," Raymond said. "Labouf's with him."

Reynolds tugged at the lock.

"Leave that alone," Jackson said.

Reynolds began to beat out a frantic rhythm on the top of the locker.

"Alabama, when you going out to Tom Light?" Raymond asked.

"Don't know," Jackson said.

"We want to talk to him."

"You know where he lives."

"There's dinks out there. We'll be safe if we go with you."

"You'd get wasted."

"Tom Light can bring back Jimi."

"You don't really believe that shit?"

"The slopes believe it. Light can do it. Does it with his starlight."

"Light wastes dinks with it. Don't raise anybody."

"That's not what we heard. Yards say he can do it. Dinks in Vung Tau say he can do it."

"You heard a bunch of fucking lies."

"He can do it."

"You're as stupid as the fucking dinks. Get out of here!"

Reynolds stopped beating on the footlocker. He picked up his M-16 and began to play it.

"Never saw so many locks," Raymond said, tugging at one of the padlocks. "You got the key?"

"No," Jackson said. "You better leave that alone. Labouf said he'd kill anyone who fucks with it."

Raymond whistled and dropped the lock.

"Labouf got drugs in here?"

"Just letters. Personal stuff."

"Think he'd let us watch him open it?"

"Shit, no."

"You ask him, Alabama. Tell the money man we'll help him guard it."

"He's no money man. Get off that locker. Don't come down here again. You do, I'll personally kick your ass."

They stood up and Jackson pushed the footlocker back under the cot. They would be back, and when they killed Labouf to get his money, they might kill him too.

"Tell the money man we'll come again," Raymond said as they left the TOC. "Can't hide the smell of money."

CHAPTER

12

JACKSON, SITTING WITH THE RADIO on the TOC's overhead cover, heard the pop of enemy AK-47 rifle fire from the ridge and saw green tracers shoot up into the night sky. He wondered if a patrol had been ambushed by the NVA.

"Jackson, you there?" the words came out of the handset, hissed instead of spoken.

Jackson gulped air. "It's me."

"I'm on the rock," Light said. "They got me cornered."

Now a light machine gun was firing in short bursts.

"I'll call Major Hale," Jackson said.

Light spoke quickly, "No, you get'em on the guns quick. Fire on my position."

"We'll kill you too," Jackson said.

"My position, quick!" Light said.

A long burst of green tracers came from above the rock and an explosion which sounded to Jackson like a frag.

"Your position?" Jackson said.

Light did not reply.

Jackson slid off the bunker and ran for the mortar pits.

The mortar squad lived in a tent ten meters away from the nearest gun pit.

Jackson yelled into the tent, "Fire mission!"

"Shit, man," a voice came out of a darkness which was lit only by a single candle. "FDC ain't called from the TOC."

"He didn't call fire direction control," Jackson said. "He called me."

They were all stoned. He could smell it.

"They'll kill him!" he yelled, now inside the tent, wondering how these men were going to save Light.

"Fuck it—oh, I'm so fucking short," a soldier moaned. He lay sprawled face down on a cot, so stoned he could barely talk.

"Five fucking days," the soldier continued.

"We'll catch Green's shorts," a soldier said.

The stoned men of the mortar squad began to giggle, all except Leander who wore his pith helmet pushed back on his head.

"Who you talking about?" Leander asked.

"Light, they'll kill him!" Jackson said.

Leander laughed and said, "Nobody'll kill that fucker. I told you stay away from us."

"Go—the rock—come on!" Jackson said, pulling one of the giggling men to his feet. "Get out there or I'll kill you!"

For the first time Jackson noticed the man was dressed in a suit with wide lapels and bell-bottomed trousers.

"Hey dude, don't mess with my threads," the man said. And then to Leander, "Light's bro gonna bring down the bad shit on us."

Jackson realized the soldier had probably been to Hong Kong on R&R and was showing off his new, custom-made suit to the squad. Three other suits hung from a rope stretched across the top of the tent, the suits encased in clear plastic bags.

Leander leaped across the tent and pushed Jackson up against the sandbags stacked along the wall. Jackson felt the point of a bayonet at his throat.

"Fucker, I'm gonna kill your goddamn honky ass!" Leander said.

"My position, quick," Light's voice came out of the handset, no longer whispered but strong and urgent.

Everyone on the squad heard it. Leander lowered the bayonet.

"They'll kill him—come on—the guns!" Jackson said.

Led by Leander, the squad ran out of the tent for the pits. The men began carrying ammo up from a bunker.

"Where?" Leander said.

"The rock, on the ridge," Jackson said.

Leander called fire direction control on the land line, and in a few seconds he had a setting for the gunsight and a number for the charges which he yelled to his gunners. As one man sighted the gun on the candy-striped aiming stakes, the men were cutting charges, pulling off the thin white squares of TNT stacked at the base of each shell like a deck of cards.

"Tom Light, Tom Light," Jackson said into the handset.

From the ridge came a long burst from the light machine gun, followed by the heavy crack of Light's .303.

"Tell that fucker to keep his head down," Leander yelled at Jackson.

"Tom Light, rounds on the way," Jackson said into the handset.

Leander checked the sight and gave the signal for the other guns to start firing.

Men began dropping shells down the tubes, and Jackson counted fifteen shells in the air. They waited for the first impact, seeing the flash on the ridge, followed a few seconds later by the crack of the high explosive. Then the others were falling.

"Add fifty," Light's calm voice came out of the handset.

Fifteen more shells went out.

"Left, Twenty-five," Light said.

The guns fired. Jackson noticed Green standing atop one of the sandbag walls that surrounded the mortar pit.

"Five days," Green yelled. "Tom Light I'll fuck your sister."

And Green, stoned out of his mind, continued to laugh and yell from the top of the wall.

"Add one hundred, airburst, they're running," Light said.

"Set'em for six seconds," Leander yelled.

Again the gunners sighted the tubes and cut the charges. A gunner set a timer on the nose of each shell which would set off a charge to explode it before it hit the ground, spraying shrapnel downward. The soldier worked quickly, and Jackson thought the man missed one. As the crewmen began dropping the shells down the tube, Jackson watched the shell the soldier had not touched.

Then as a soldier started to drop the shell down the tube, Jackson knew that time had not been set.

"Wait—" Jackson said, stepping forward, already realizing that it was too late. "No time!"

The shell disappeared out of the soldiers's hands.

"Short round!" Leander yelled and everyone along with Jackson hit the ground.

Jackson looked up and saw a soldier stand up and try to pull Green down off the wall.

A great roar and bright flash filled up the night as the shell went off twenty meters out of the tube, the time set on zero. Jackson looked up and saw the soldier who had been trying to pull Green down running across the pit on the stumps of his legs. Green still stood on the wall laughing. The man ran into the sandbag wall and collapsed, lying there screaming with a strange high-pitched wail that made Jackson want to laugh. But instead Jackson threw up.

"We got'em," Light's voice came over the handset.

"More rounds?" Jackson said, spitting to clear his mouth.

"Negative, it was beautiful," Light said. "Not a whole dink out there."

Jackson replaced the handset. Leander was kneeling beside the soldier who lay on his back at the base of the sandbag wall screaming for his mother. The sweet scent of blood filled the pit.

One of the men went for a medic.

"Shut up!" Leander screamed at the soldier. "Shut the fuck up!"

The soldier continued to scream. As the men tied tourniquets around the stumps, his screams turned to animal-like groans. Then the groans stopped. Jackson was grateful for that.

"I'm so fucking short," Green said, still standing on the wall.

The squad ignored him.

"Green's shorts didn't do Calvin no good," a soldier said.

"Light's bad luck stronger than that man's shorts," another said.

"Maybe the major'll write it up as enemy action so his family can have a medal," a third said.

Leander stood to one side, looking out toward the ridge.

"I'm sorry—" Jackson began, walking toward him.

"Fucker, you stay away from me. I'm squad leader. I should've checked. Williams is fucked up enough when he's straight. I should've known he'd fuck up, I should've known," Leander said.

"It wasn't your fault," Jackson said.

"Light, you cocksucker!" Leander screamed out toward the ridge. "Sitting out there laughing at us. Put willie peter on that mo-'fucker."

And Leander opened a cardboard tube which contained the mortar shell and began stripping charges off it.

"Be cool," a soldier said. "You saw what happened to Calvin. Light always brings down the shit on people."

They wrestled Leander to the ground.

"Get out of here!" one of them yelled to Jackson.

He walked off past the mortar squad tent, large holes torn in the canvas by the shrapnel. At the mortar pits the men were still arguing with Leander over dropping white phosphorus on Light.

Jackson pressed the transmission bar and said, "Tom Light, Tom Light."

Only white noise hissed out of the handset, but he kept calling.

"Hey, Marcus, your suits are fucked," a soldier yelled from the tent.

Marcus ran past Jackson. A few seconds later, Jackson saw Marcus and another soldier using a flashlight to look at the suits they had laid out on a cot. Jackson noticed Marcus was wearing a white dress shirt and a lavender tie.

"Goddamn, ruined, all of them," Marcus said. "I was going to be the best-dressed dude in D.C."

Marcus stuck his hand through a shrapnel hole.

"Ruined, fucked, wasted," Marcus continued.

"Least you ain't dead," the other said. "I told you to leave'em at Pleiku."

"It's Light. He might as well have come in here himself with a shotgun and blowed'em full of holes." Marcus said.

Jackson felt sick again, but when he knelt on the ground with his head down, he found nothing was left in his stomach.

One man dead, he thought. Dinks blown to pieces out at the rock. Marcus worrying about this fucking suits. Tom Light in love with the war.

"I'm going to be short," Jackson muttered as he walked toward the bunker. "I'm going to be short."

CHAPTER

13

BY THE BIG ROCK at night, Jackson sat with Tom Light under a poncho they had thrown over themselves, the air rank with the scent of decaying leaves. While Light held a flashlight, Jackson wrote a letter. Jackson had walked out the gate again. Hale would be mad when he returned, but Jackson knew there was nothing the major could do.

"Starlight is fucking up," Light said after he signed the letter. "You saved my ass. Didn't know they were coming. Keep seeing the weird shit in it. Don't need to see the weird shit. I gotta know. You saw it, first day I was here."

"I didn't see," Jackson said.

"I know what you saw," Light said. "It's that man the dinks brought in. They call him the Tiger. Works up in the fucking trees. Hard to pin down. He's the one who blocked the trail. But he ain't that good. Shit, I can kill him without the starlight."

"You'll waste him," Jackson said. "Easy."

"Easy?" Light asked.

"Sure." Jackson said.

Light sighed, an ancient sound, and said, "With the Tiger out there nothing is gonna be easy."

"You'll kill him," Jackson said.

"Maybe he's like me. Maybe he's not so easy to kill."

Jackson sucked in a deep breath at Light's concern over the enemy sniper.

"You can kill him anytime you want," Jackson said, forgetting to whisper and listening to the sound of his words echo off the rock.

Light held up his hand for silence.

"I didn't say I couldn't do it," Light said. "Won't be easy is what I meant."

Now Jackson felt better, safe again.

"They're coming in to mortar the firebase tonight," Light said. "I saw it in the scope. Cover for a probe. It'll be good hunting. Maybe the Tiger'll be there."

"We should tell the TOC," Jackson said.

"Fuck those base camp soldiers."

"Hale will have my ass."

It was scary Light could see the future in the starlight, Jackson thought to himself. But even more scary was that there were times when Light did not know. Tonight he knew, and Jackson felt safe.

Jackson followed Light through the rain forest. They crossed a trail, and Jackson expected they would take it. Instead, Light led him through vegetation so thick Jackson could see only a few feet in front of him. Light disappeared and Jackson froze, feeling the dark jungle close in on him. Light might walk off and leave him. It could happen.

But after what seemed to Jackson like a long time, Light walked back out of the tangle of trees and vines.

"Grab hold of my sweater," Light whispered. "Move when I do. Don't make noise."

With the bottom of Light's sweater wrapped around his fingers, Jackson followed him through the jungle. Light took a few steps, stood motionless for a time, and then moved forward again. He repeated this hunter's pattern over and over.

Jackson felt like he had dived into a lake at night. The jungle was not like scrub and small trees of the area around the firebase. Here the big trees shut out the light from the stars and moon. He felt smothered by the darkness and searched for a clear spot in the canopy where he could see the sky again. The leaves were wet from a rain storm earlier that day, the ground soggy under his feet.

Wet, wet, wet, he thought. Rotten with mold. Waiting to eat my body if Light makes a mistake and gets me killed.

Gradually the land rose, and Light began to walk much faster. Jackson kept getting tangled in vines. Then the ground slanted almost straight up, and they pulled themselves up the slope on tree limbs and vines. At the top they crossed a trail, and this time Light took it. After walking on it a few feet, Jackson guessed the reason why. It was a trail made by animals, not men. At several places they crawled along it as the trail tunneled through the underbrush.

When the trail disappeared in a thick stand of bamboo, they forced their way through the narrow places between the shoots. Light stopped and motioned for Jackson to crawl up beside him.

"We wait here," Light said. "Don't move. Don't go to sleep."

Jackson lay motionless on the soft carpet of dead bamboo leaves. The mosquitoes swarmed about him, his insect repellent long ago sweated off. He thought he could feel leeches crawling on his body under his fatigues.

To Jackson it seemed they lay there for hours. The sounds of the night animals and the H&I fire from the firebase made keeping his eyes open easy. Finally Light tapped him on the shoulder.

"Slow and careful now," Light said. "Follow me."

Jackson looked at the luminescent dial of his watch. It was two o'clock. They crawled slowly, the bamboo thicket eventually thinning out. Jackson saw a place ahead where the darkness was not so thick.

Not being afraid was a strange sensation. But what if something happened to Light, if the men Light was going to shoot killed him instead, if the Tiger won his battle with Tom Light? Jackson gulped air.

Light motioned for him to stay. It was hard to see Light move at all, but gradually his dark shape was gone. In ten minutes by Jackson's watch, Light returned.

"Don't move, be quiet," Light again whispered in his ear.

They lay still for a long time, Jackson not daring to raise his head to look at his watch.

I should've stayed on my listening post, Jackson thought.

"Move when I move," Light whispered in his ear.

Jackson kept pace with Light as they crawled across the open space. Light took his time doing it. It felt like they were crawling about a meter an hour. He turned his head and looked up at the stars, no longer feeling smothered by the jungle. Light stopped, motioning for Jackson to crawl up beside him. Then Light offered him the rifle, and Jackson took it.

They were on a hill, the ground falling away before them to form a bowl-shaped depression full of elephant grass covered with patches of a thin, white mist. Jackson hesitated for a moment, afraid of what he might see, but then put his eye to the scope. Along the tree line he saw in the green glow of the starlight a squad of NVA carrying light mortars, some with the tubes and others with the baseplates and shells. Light took the rifle back.

"Lay still, wait until they set up," Light said.

Jackson took a deep breath, worried about the noise he made as he did it. Sweat ran down his face, and his whole body tingled with fear. He wanted to shout, to jump up and charge the NVA, anything but lie on the ground and wait. Yet at the same time he wished he could burrow underground like a mole to hide. He felt envy for the NVA and their tunnels. Somewhere close by was surely a tunnel, a cave, a place to hide.

Hide, he thought to himself. Hide deep down in the earth.

But hiding was not all right. To run, to hide, was to break the rules. He decided he would lie very still with his face pressed to the ground while Tom Light did the fighting. That was not running and not fighting but something in between. If Light needed him to fight, he would fight.

I hope I fight good, he thought to himself.

Jackson heard something move in the grass below. The sound came closer and breathing hard a soldier walked up the steep slope toward them. Jackson felt Light's hand on the back of his head as the sniper slowly pressed Jackson's face to the ground.

Lie still and be like a patch of vines or a rotting log, Jackson thought.

Closer and closer the sound came.

He's going to step on me, Jackson thought.

Instead of being confused his head was clear, the possibility of the soldier stepping on the middle of his back occupying his entire attention.

I'm not going to be able to move when he does, Jackson thought. The grass swished against the soldier's uniform. He was right on top of them now. Jackson wanted to scream but doubted that he could get enough air into his lungs to yell. With teeth clenched, he tried to silently draw air into his burning lungs.

Suddenly the sound stopped. At any moment he expected to feel a knife at his throat. Light might decide to lie still in the darkness and allow the enemy soldier to kill him. A series of rustling sounds came from just beyond his head, only a meter or so away. Then it was quiet. He gradually became conscious of Light moving past him, moving so slowly that as Jackson watched Light with his peripheral vision, he found it hard to be certain Light was moving. But when he saw Light's foot slide past and disappear, he knew Tom Light was going to kill the enemy soldier.

A faint popping sound came from directly in front of Jackson. The soldier had farted. He smelled the sour stink.

What if the dink decides to take a break from his listening post to beat off, Jackson thought. And what if Light chooses that moment for the kill, lopping it off at the instant of his enemy's pleasure? Jackson had to try hard to keep from laughing. Crazy, he told himself. You're as crazy as Tom Light.

Someone sighed like a man might as he sat down in an easy chair after a long day of work. Then there was a faint bubbling sound and the sweet smell of blood like in the mortar pits when the soldier had lost his legs. Light reappeared beside him.

"They're setting up below," Light said. "They'll be making noise and won't notice us. If they see any movement up here, they'll think it's their own security."

Jackson lifted his head and saw close enough to reach out and touch the body of the NVA soldier. The man lay on his back with his mouth wide open. Even in the dark Jackson could see a dark stain of blood on the front of the man's uniform. Had Light taken a trophy? Jackson thought. No way to tell, the man's lower body hidden by the grass.

Jackson did not want to look too close. He felt a great sense of calm. He was safe out in the bush with Light, safe as he would have been home in bed back in Alabama. Soon Light would teach him all the tricks. Maybe he could become as good as Tom Light.

How would it have felt to have killed the soldier? he thought.

Light had the rifle to his shoulder, lying prone on the ground. Jackson wondered if Light was going to begin killing NVA. Light lowered the rifle.

"Here, look," he whispered in Jackson's ear.

Through the scope Jackson watched the soldiers assembling tubes to the baseplates. Others were digging holes in a line along the edge of the field.

"They'll hide in the pits and then start dropping rounds," Light whispered. "They'll get twenty or thirty rounds in the air before the firebase has time to shoot back or send out gunships. Soon as they start dropping rounds down the tubes, I'll start shooting."

Light took the rifle, leaving Jackson to stare into the darkness wondering how he was going to shoot what he couldn't see.

Thonk, thonk, thonk, thonk. Jackson heard the 82-millimeter mortar rounds begin to go out of the tubes. The firing continued, and he heard the crack of the impacts on the firebase. Light's rifle boomed. Jackson raised his M-16.

"No," Light whispered. "Watch behind us."

Jackson stared at the dark mass of jungle while Light continued to shoot. The NVA shot too, and he listened to the pop of the AK-47s. They were firing wild, a burst of automatic fire ripping through the trees high above them.

I'm not afraid, Jackson thought to himself.

He smiled as he flattened himself against the ground. Light would kill them all. As long as no one saw the muzzle flashes of Light's rifle, they would be all right.

Light stopped shooting. Jackson had counted ten shots and guessed that ten enemy were dead. The mortaring had stopped.

"Move slow," Light whispered. "Don't make noise."

He followed Light into the big trees, Light moving much faster than when they had approached the field. Once inside the canopy Light stopped.

"You did good," Light said.

"Thanks," Jackson said.

"They ran."

"The probe?"

"Finished. No cover for it now."

Light made a faint popping sound with his lips to show what little chance the probe had now.

"Was the Tiger there?" Jackson asked.

"No, but he's close," Light said. "I can feel him."

Jackson gulped air at the thought of the Tiger, who was almost as good as Light.

Going back, they walked instead of crawling. When they crossed a trail, Light took it.

Light knew, Jackson thought. Light was crazy, but he knew when it was safe and would keep him alive.

Jackson felt excited watching Light kill the NVA. It was almost as if he had been pulling the trigger himself, the kills his as much as Light's.

Suddenly the jungle around them was torn apart by a huge sound. Jackson felt a pressure wave roll over him and things small and hissing rushed past his head. A machine gun began firing at them off to Jackson's right, the muzzle flashes barely visible through the thick cover, the bullets popping and snapping as they hit leaves and branches. Jackson felt himself falling, not really conscious that he had willed himself to fall, and pressed his body close to the wet clay of the trail, listening to the whine of bullets over his head. Boom, click, click; boom, click, click. He heard Light shooting the rifle and working the action to chamber another round. Jackson raised his head and through the smoke left from the explosions saw Light, who was still standing on the trail, fire one final shot into the jungle.

A man screamed. In return there was a single shot that went between Jackson and Light, making a ripping sound in the air as it passed. Jackson knew it was one of the heavy steel-jacketed bullets like the ones Light used. Then it was quiet. Jackson wondered if he had been hit somewhere, hit so bad that there was no pain for the present. Sometimes that happened to soldiers.

"They're running," Light said, kneeling beside him. "You, OK?" Jackson felt his body carefully, first his balls, then head and stomach and arms and legs.

"I'm alive," Jackson said. "What was it?"

"Claymores," Light said. "Two or three. Rigged up with trip wires. Starlight didn't fuck up. It was me. My fault for walking the trail. I know better."

Jackson remembered about claymore mines from infantry training and tried to recall just how many steel pellets each mine contained. Six or seven hundred he thought, maybe a thousand.

My rifle, Jackson thought.

His rifle was gone, and he remembered that something had torn it out of his hands when the claymores went off. Down on his hands and knees, he searched for it in the darkness until with relief he felt the barrel with his fingertips. But when he picked it up, he discovered that the claymore pellets had shredded the plastic stock. Jackson began to shake, his whole body trembling. Light was alive and he was alive. How?

"I hit three of them," Light said. "Did you hear the Tiger's big gun?"

"What?" Jackson said, not hearing all of Light's words, still running his shaking fingers over the place where the stock had been joined to the receiver.

"His big gun."

"The Tiger?"

"Yeah. Maybe he's using a Chinese night scope or a captured starlight. Only way he could've pinned me down at the rock that night. Only way he could have come so close tonight. But tonight I knew he was there. Had his chance and missed. I'll kill him soon."

"How did the claymores miss?" Jackson asked, forcing the words out with difficulty and choking as he spoke. "How did the machine gun miss?"

Light said, "I was here."

"We should be dead," Jackson said, hoping Light would not notice the shaking. At any moment he expected his teeth to start chattering.

Then Light's hand was on his arm, the fingers strong and steady. Jackson stopped shaking as Light pulled him to his feet.

"No dink ambush is ever going to kill me," Light said.

For the first time since he had arrived in country, Jackson was certain he was going to survive the war.

Light can do fucking anything, he thought to himself. I'm going to live.

CHAPTER

14

LIGHT BEGAN KILLING NVA. Patrols found the bodies out in the bush, not mutilated this time, all with a single bullet hole in the head. Soon attacks on the fence almost stopped. Wire was being strung, and Hale was in a good mood. Jackson no longer saw him working at the map tripod, plotting his attack on the Holiday Inn.

Jackson was in the TOC. Labouf had just come on duty for his shift on the big radio, and Hale was talking with II Corps about progress on the fence.

"Goddamn, but Tom Light is one fine sniper," Hale said switching off the mike.

"I'd be charging Two Corps a hundred dollars a head if I was Light," Labouf said.

"He going to stay out there until he's run every one of them back over into Laos," Hale said.

Labouf leaned far back in his chair and said, "Yeah, in a few weeks it'll be just like stateside."

During the days that followed Light continued to kill the enemy and the engineers strung wire in the Cunt. For Jackson it was a good time. He lounged about on the sandbags during the day and thought of boarding the plane that was going to take him home to Loretta.

Then Reynolds & Raymond quit shadowing Labouf.

"Alabama, you seen R&R?" Labouf asked Jackson.

"No."

"I liked it better when I knew where they were," Labouf said. The next time Jackson saw Reynolds & Raymond was when he came out of the TOC one evening just before sunset. They were standing under the tower with so many cloth bandoleers for M-16 magazines slung across their chests they couldn't lower their arms. Clusters of frags were hooked to their web gear. Raymond wore a K-Bar fighting knife on his belt along with a bayonet, and Reynolds carried several LAWs slung over his shoulder.

"Expecting trouble?" Jackson asked. "Gonna shoot those LAW rockets at NVA tanks?"

Raymond said, "No. Sappers."

They both fidgeted nervously, shifting their weight from one foot to the other. Reynolds played his M-16.

"The dinks got a tunnel," Raymond continued, talking very fast. "Can put your ear to the ground and hear'em digging. When they dig through, we'll be waiting. Been hunting those dink tunnel diggers all over 'Nam. About time we'd get ready to waste them, we'd get shipped out. Been to Cheo Reo, Dak To, Bong Son, An Nhon, Song Cau, Tuy Hoa, An Khe, Kontum. Jesus, there's no place in fucking Two Corps where the dinks don't have a tunnel. Seriously, this motherfucking country will collapse one day. They got it undermined. Careless fuckers. Don't keep the tunnels shored up. Shipped us out to Dak To last time. Said this place was the end of the line. We like it fine. Right, buddy?"

Raymond patted Reynolds on the shoulder. Reynolds giggled.

"We're tunnel rats," Raymond continued. "Cong killers, dink destroyers, gook greasers."

"Where're they digging?" Jackson asked.

"Over by the mortar pits," Raymond said. "Where the chaplain holds church. That short fucker. Too short for an American. Chaplain's a goddamn dink in disguise. Had plastic surgery done on his face up in Hanoi. He's been signaling to the dinks up on the ridge.

We've been watching. When he makes the cross sign during communion, it's a code. My buddy cracked it. Should get a medal.''
Reynolds grinned.

"You boys'll waste'em," Jackson said, humoring them.

"Come on ambush with us," Raymond said. "We think they'll be digging through tonight."

Reynolds sang, "You've got me blowing, blowing my mind/Is it tomorrow or just the end of time?"

"No thanks," Jackson said.

Later that night Jackson walked out of the TOC to go to the latrine. He was glad it was in the opposite direction from where Reynolds & Raymond had set up their ambush.

"Sappers!" someone yelled.

There was M-16 fire on automatic, another LAW, and the chug of a heavy machine gun from the perimeter. Red tracers crisscrossed the firebase. Jackson dropped to the ground. He did not want to be trapped in a bunker by sappers tossing satchel charges.

Maybe Reynolds & Raymond had been right. The fire was coming from a position near the mortar pits.

Another LAW went off, the rocket impacting near the TOC. Now fire from the whole perimeter was turned inward, directed at the mortar pits. Flares went up, and he saw men crawling across the compound. Then the fire from the mortar pits stopped.

Jackson got up and ran for the TOC. Leander and Hale were there. Leander had taken off his pith helmet and held it with one hand by his side. Labouf was at the radio.

"You find those bastards!" Hale shouted at Leander. "You make sure they don't have weapons again when they are on this firebase. We go over into Laos, they'll be walking point." Then Hale continued, "Get rid of that fucking helmet."

"Yes, sir," Leander said, putting on the helmet before he left the TOC.

Hale went into his room.

"Fucking R&R have stepped in the shit," Labouf said and grinned. "Won't be following me around no more. Leander said they started shooting at the mortar crew when his guys got called out on a fire mission. Shit, R&R got one half of this fucking place shooting at the other. Lucky no one got killed.''

"What's Hale mean about going to Laos?''

"Aw, that fucking crazy Morton at Two Corps it always on his ass to go over there. Nothing'll come of it now that the engineers are stringing wire.''

Jackson took the radio and went up on the roof of the TOC. The flares had all burned out and the firebase was quite. He set the radio on Light's frequency and waited.

"Tom Light, Tom Light,'' Jackson said into the handset, thinking of what might happen if Hale took the battalion over into Laos.

White noise hissed from the handset. Jackson lay back on the sandbags and closed his eyes. He began to think of home, how good it was going to be to walk out of the house on a summer morning and go to the barn to feed the horses his father kept.

"Jackson,'' Light's voice came out of the handset.

"I'm here,'' Jackson said.

"I can't use the starlight no more. Don't want to see the weird shit. Know what's gonna happen to the troops. But don't know what'll happen to me.''

Jackson gasped for breath and said, "There's nothing in the scope?''

"You keep your head down. You'll be all right.''

"What about the Tiger?''

"You'll be all right. I'm thinking about going over into Laos. There's an abandoned city up there. No need to look through the starlight there. No war.''

"You stay here. Remember your mother's heart. There'll be your mail.''

Light paused and replied, "Maybe I'll stay, but I ain't looking through the starlight. No more killing.''

"I'll write your letters. I'll come out.''

Then Jackson released the transmission bar and waited for Light to talk. Nothing came out of the handset but white noise. He was gone.

Jackson took a deep, slow breath to try to calm himself but failed and ended up lying on his back gasping. Light maybe gone, walking to Laos. Labouf's money could get them out. Bribe a chopper pilot and fly to Saigon. From there to Sweden. A year or two to learn the language. Money in the bank. It would be easy. But he couldn't. Just something to dream about. Even if he had the plane ticket in hand he could not run. The people at home: Loretta, his parents, Uncle Frank, and the cousins scattered throughout the country expected him to stay, to die if necessary. He wished he could be with Light, buddies, still soldiers, walking the jungle into Laos, eating deer roasted over a fire, drinking from the mountain streams, Loretta haunting his dreams at night.

CHAPTER

15

WHEN THE TIGER SHOT the Jesus nut off a chopper the main rotor blades went flying off into the bush. As the ship crashed just outside the wire, the fuel tanks going up with a black, oily whoosh, Jackson knew that without Tom Light it was going to be very bad at the firebase. Jackson had not heard from Light on the radio and hoped he had not gone over into Laos.

Labouf said, "We're all going to die."

"I'll be safe. Me and Light have a deal," Jackson said, only half-believing it himself, but it could not hurt to say it.

"Jesus, Alabama, leave that alone," Labouf said.

And it soon began to look as if Labouf was right. The Tiger shot guards out of the tower, door gunners out of choppers, and men at the piss tubes. He shot a chaplain as the priest was placing the host in a soldier's mouth during a communion service. Always it was one shot, and he never missed. No one was ever sure exactly where the fire was coming from. When the soldiers heard the distant crack of his rifle they would pause for a moment and wonder who had just died.

Hale called in airstrikes on the ridge, the only possible place the fire could be coming from. For three days the bombing went on, mostly napalm. Every day the Tiger killed a man. Then the air force gave up and went away, telling Hale it was the infantry's job to flush out snipers. They refused his request for an arclight.

"I got it figured out," Labouf said.

"You're going to stay in the TOC the rest of the war," Jackson said.

Labouf laughed and said, "No, you're safe as long as you act normal."

And everyone soon lived by Labouf's theory. Commonplace targets were safe. The Tiger never shot a man unless the soldier's death was likely to cause laughter among the living. When the Tiger shot a man who was not wearing his fatigue jacket but was doing nothing else unusual, everyone on the firebase began wearing his jacket, no matter how hot the day was. They all adopted a stiff way of moving like people who had suddenly found themselves on stage but were not used to being there.

"I've made a map," Labouf said.

"Of what?" Jackson asked.

"The Tiger's kills."

They were in the TOC, and Labouf spread a sheet of paper out on Hale's map tripod.

"See, there's a pattern," Labouf explained. "I've figured out where the safest places are. Piss tubes'll be all right for a while."

Jackson laughed and said, "We're in the safest place."

"But we gotta leave sometime. I wouldn't walk over by the mortar pits. That's the next place he's going to kill a man."

That night a mortar crewman died as he held his eye to the gunsight. Soon Labouf was selling looks at his map and the predictions that went with them for ten dollars, payable in advance.

"Haven't you got enough money?" Jackson said.

"No one has enough," Labouf replied. "I'm saving lives, providing a service. I'm doing more than that fucking Hale."

Labouf was right. Hale chose to ignore the Tiger, walking about the firebase like it was business as usual and grumbling about the B-52 arclight the air force had refused to give him.

"He's saving the major for last," Labouf told Jackson.

"Light could kill that dink easy," Jackson said.

"Tom Light's gone."

"He's out there. Watching out for my ass. He's better than any map."

Labouf laughed and said, "You haven't died yet, but that don't mean he has anything to do with it. You're lucky, that's all."

You'll see, Jackson thought to himself. Tom Light would live up to his end of the bargain.

The men began to grumble that they were all doomed, that one by one the Tiger would kill them. Hale posted an extra guard at the entrance to the TOC and started sleeping with an M-60 machine gun.

Jackson has just finished talking with a radio operator at the fence about the sniper's latest kill when he heard boots on the stairs. Leander led the mortar squad into the TOC. He had the strap of the pith helmet buckled under his chin.

"Alabama, where's the major?" Leander asked.

"Asleep," Jackson said. "How'd you get in here?"

"Those guards want to live too. You wake him up."

"Come back later."

"Now."

The others hung back, letting Leander do all of the talking.

"You come back," Jackson said.

"We're not leaving until we talk to the major," Leander said.

Jackson opened the door of the tiny room where Hale slept at the rear of the bunker. Hale was asleep, snoring. But when Jackson whispered his name, Hale sat upright. His body was in darkness, the light from the TOC blocked by Jackson. Jackson heard Hale draw back the bolt on the machine gun.

"Who's out there?" Hale asked.

"The mortar squad."

"What do they want?"

"Talk to you, sir."

"The Tiger again?"

"Don't know."

Hale sighed and swung his legs off the cot. He was wearing his boots.

Too scared to sleep with his boots off, Jackson thought. Maybe as scared as me. Hale walked out of the room with the M-60 under his arm, still sleepy, blinking at the light.

"Soldier, don't you ever come down here again," Hale said to Leander.

"Tiger gonna kill us all," Leander said.

"I've got patrols out after him," Hale said.

"What's Light doing?" Leander asked.

"Shit, how am I supposed to know," Hale said talking fast.

"You get him to hunting," Leander said. "He can kill the Tiger."

"Soldier, you're going to be out in the bush humping a baseplate if you don't watch out."

"I ain't humping nothing for you," Leander said.

Here was the mutiny Hale kept worrying about.

"You can be on the next patrol that goes out after the Tiger," Hale said. "Get out of here. I don't want to see any of you in here again."

"You can't let my men get picked off and do nothing," Leander said.

"I thought you men were scared of Light?"

"We want him out in the bush hunting, not here."

"He hasn't been killing," Hale said. "Maybe he's taking a break. The dinks haven't been fucking with the fence."

"He knows that fucking fence is going nowhere," Leander said. "Goddamn fucking generals."

"That fence is going up, soldier. Don't matter to the army whether you like it or not," Hale said, talking fast.

Then he turned to Jackson, "You heard from Light?"

Jackson said, "He talked about going to live with the mountain people. He—"

But a soldier broke in and said, "You get him back, Major."

"Probably dead," Hale said.

Leander shook his head and said, "No way to kill Tom Light."

"Jackson tries to make contact with him every day," Hale said.

Leander said, "You get Light to kill the Tiger. We're not gonna get wasted alone."

"All of you, out!" Hale yelled, his finger on the trigger of the machine gun.

They shuffled their feet, glared at Hale, and left.

"Leander, I see you with that helmet one more time and I'm going to think you're a gook," Hale said. "Hope I have an M-60 in my hands."

"I'd have a better chance of staying alive if I was a dink," Leander said as he disappeared up the stairs.

"Go out there, you bastard!" Hale shouted after him.

The only reply was the sound of Leander's boots on the stairs.

Jackson continued to call Light on the radio but received no response. The Tiger began to shoot men digging post holes, and work on the fence stopped. The engineer CO told Hale he was not going to string any more wire until the sniper was flushed out.

Hale sent out patrols to look for Light. Some did not return, and others came back with nothing to report except contact with the enemy. The major posted new guards at the entrance to the TOC. Now Jackson did not like to work in the TOC while the major was there, for he expected the men were going to frag Hale at the first opportunity.

Jackson had just come off pulling a shift on the big radio when the tower guard called to report movement at the big rock. He followed Hale up into the tower.

Hale snatched the glasses out of the tower guard's hand and through an observation loophole set in the sandbags focused them on the rock.

"Where?" Hale asked.

"Right in front of the big rock, Sir," the guard replied. "He's building something. I think it's Light."

"It's a dink," Hale said.

The guard said, "No sir, Tom Light."

"By God, it is Light," Hale said. "What the hell is he doing?"

"Cutting down trees," the guard replied.

Hale handed the glasses to Jackson and said, "Look, see what your man's doing."

Jackson saw Light dragging a small tree across the open space. He stopped and began lopping off branches with a machete.

He was always out there, Jackson thought. That's why the Tiger didn't get me.

"What's he doing?" Hale asked again.

"Don't know," Jackson replied.

Hale said, "He's already run the Tiger back into Laos."

"Light'll waste him," the tower guard said, mounting the fire-step and looking over the top of the sandbags.

Suddenly the guard fell back across the floor like someone had jerked him with a rope, the crack of the rifle reaching them a moment later. Jackson crawled over to the soldier to help but already knew the man was dead.

"He's finished. See what Light's doing," Hale said.

Jackson found he could not move, his breath coming in short gasps.

"Move, soldier," Hale said.

Jackson crawled over to the loophole. When he picked up the glasses, he hoped they were broken, but they were all right.

"Move!" Hale said.

With one hand, Jackson placed the glasses in the loophole. He expected, hoped, the Tiger would shoot them.

"They can't look by themselves," Hale said.

Jackson rose to his knees and turned the knob to focus the glasses on the rock.

"Light still there?" Hale asked.

"Yeah," Jackson replied.

"What's he doing?"

"Cutting trees."

"And the Tiger is killing my men."

Hale cursed Light long and eloquently.

Light built a hooch, a small hut roofed with leaves. He spent most of his time at the hut sitting in the doorway with his back to the firebase. At night there was a glow from the hut as if he had built a small fire to keep away the mosquitoes. But nobody wanted to look at the hut for long because that meant exposing themselves to fire from the Tiger.

Jackson tried to contact Light on the radio but got no answer, so Hale sent out a patrol to take Light a new walkie-talkie and instruct him to start hunting again. Hale was unable to sit still as he waited for the patrol to make contact with Light. He tried to work at his map tripod but ended up pacing back and forth. Finally the patrol called him on the radio.

"What did he say?" Hale asked the lieutenant.

"Says he's not killing anymore. Going to sit in his hut until the war is over," the lieutenant replied.

Light stayed at his hut, and the Tiger continued to harass the firebase. He shot another guard out of the tower, killed two more mortar crewmen, and shot the glass out of a periscope the men were using on the perimeter.

Then Leander, still wearing his pith helmet, asked to see Hale. Hale had him report to the TOC. Leander came alone.

"Ain't putting my men out on the guns for the Tiger to kill no more," Leander said.

"You and your men will go to jail," Hale said.

"Least we'll be alive in LBJ. You send Jackson out. He's Light's main man. He can talk to him. Everything'll be cool then."

Jackson took a deep breath.

"Jackson's getting paid to be my RTO, not to go out in the bush," Hale said, talking fast. "You think you run this firebase. Think you can give my men orders. Jackson'll never go out as long as I'm in command."

"One day you'll get wasted," Leander said. "That'll be how the report'll read. Major got wasted by the Tiger."

"Get out of here!" Hale shouted. "Get out of my sight!"

"Yeah, you're the major," Leander said. "Long as you're here we got to do what you say."

Leander left the TOC.

Jackson wanted to be out in the bush with Light. Any night now the frag would bounce down the steps of the TOC. One of the guards posted at the entrance might do it himself.

Then a navy captain and a lieutenant commander appeared in the TOC. They told Hale they had hitched a ride on a chopper to the firebase to see some of the war. The officers wore stateside fatigues and black baseball caps with gold braid on the bills.

"Nothing much to see here," Hale said.

"They told us in Pleiku a firefight was usually going on up here," the captain said.

Hale said, "Rear areas get a distorted picture of us. I can have you choppered over to firebase Mary Lou. Lots of action up there."

But the captain decided to spend the night. Hale tried to persuade them to change into jungle fatigues along with steel pots and flak jackets, but the captain refused.

"We're just here to observe," he said. "We'll stay out of the way."

"We've got this problem with a sniper. He likes unusual targets. You're dressed different from the rest of the men. Be safer if I found you some fatigues. Sniper couldn't tell you from the enlisted men," Hale said.

The captain said, "No, thanks. We keep our heads down. Watch you kill him."

When Labouf heard about the naval officers he laughed and said, "Those guys are finished."

And Jackson agreed.

The captain and the lieutenant commander came back down into the TOC after dark to wait for some action. Labouf waited until Hale was gone then came down to try to sell the officers a look at his map. They laughed and dismissed him as a case of combat fatigue. Labouf went over the the map tripod and began to write something on his map. Jackson was surprised the navy men were still alive. The captain began to grumble that there was nothing going on.

Hale returned and said, "Jackson, call up the mortar squad and have'em fire some H&I. We'll go up in the tower and watch."

They had already left the TOC by the time Jackson got Leander on the land line.

"Not unless a patrol is in trouble," Leander said.

Jackson sat in front of the radio and waited for Hale to call on the land line from the tower. The telephone buzzed.

"Why aren't they firing?" Hale asked.

"Leander won't. Only if a patrol needs support."

Hale came down from the tower and argued with Leander on the land line. The naval officers were amused.

"That man needs a few months in the brig," the captain said.

Hale said, "He'll fire those rounds if I have to hold a pistol to his head."

They all went up out of the TOC. But no sooner had they cleared the stairway than Hale, the lieutenant commander, and the guard came half-running and half-crawling down the stairs, dragging the body of the captain behind them.

Labouf whispered in Jackson's ear, "Now you'll be going out. Some admiral is going to be pissed."

And Labouf lit the edge of the map with his lighter. He dropped it to the ground where it quickly burned. Labouf rubbed the ashes into the dirt with his boot.

"Got money I can't spend and no way to make more."

Not long after the chopper carrying the body of the captain left, General Morton called Hale on the radio.

"Can't you secure your area from snipers?" Morton said.

Jackson left the radio but stayed close enough to hear.

"The air force wouldn't give me an arclight," Hale replied.

Morton said, "You don't need an arclight for one goddamn sniper. Now the navy is raising hell with me. Some of your men told that lieutenant commander you let a sniper shoot up your camp at will. And what's this about your mortar section refusing to fight."

"That's not true," Hale said. "My men do what I tell them. We've had a problem with a sniper. I've had airstrikes. I've sent out patrols. If I could have an arclight—"

"Goddammit, Hale, you're not going to get an arclight unless the enemy is attacking in strength. What you're going to do is personally take out a patrol and kill that sniper. Major Williams told me he's had to stop work on the fence. Why wasn't I told? You're there to protect the engineers. That's your only mission. Good God, man, did those navy men see the fence?''

"No, sir, they didn't," Hale said.

"You deny it's there if the navy starts asking questions. What you're doing is classified, understand. I want results up there. You get me results and there'll be a good report on you. A promotion. Maybe colonel."

"I'll take care of the sniper. We'll start stringing wire again. You can count on me, Sir."

Hale hung up the handset and turned to Jackson.

"Get out there, Jackson," Hale said. "Take Light's mail to him. Write his letters, talk to him, hold his hand. Make sure he kills the Tiger."

CHAPTER

16

JACKSON WAS NOT AFRAID as he walked through the scrub, breathing smoothly and evenly like a man out for a walk after dinner. In his rucksack he carried .303 ammo, a new walkie-talkie, and a battery for the starlight scope. There were clouds over the mountains. Every day for the past several weeks the clouds had built up, a blue-black cliff of clouds over in Laos, but so far there had been no rain. The monsoon was late, and they all feared its arrival because it would mean a reduction in their air support.

He called Light over and over on the radio to let him know he was coming out but had received no reply.

I'll be all right, Jackson thought. Probably already knows I'm here. Won't let the Tiger waste me.

Even though he tried to walk quietly, the dead twigs and grass crackled under his boots. He entered the tree line, moving easily. The jungle had taken on a new character for him, a comfortable order instead of a random arrangement of trees and vines. It was a triple-canopy rain forest, the trees rising in three distinct layers. Walking in it was like being inside a gymnasium, that same hollow feeling. Only the patches of bamboo, the shoots growing closely

112

together, made walking difficult. At any moment he expected Light to step out from behind the buttresses of one of the huge trees.

Jackson felt no panic, experienced no fear of getting lost as he walked steadily for the big rock. Here and there were clear places where the air force had dropped bombs and napalm. But already the undergrowth had returned and had grown so thick Jackson walked around them instead of trying to push his way through. When he came out of the trees, walking on the outcropping, he saw a light ahead.

He walked into the hut, stooping at the doorway. Tom Light sat with his back against the wall, the candle burning in a holder made from an empty M-79 casing. The candle smelled like blueberries, but Jackson could still detect that jungle stink of Tom Light.

"Goddamn, the Tiger could've killed me," Jackson said. "Why'd you let him shoot up the firebase?"

"You're still alive," Light said.

"You shouldn't have let him pick us off. Didn't you see troops dying in the starlight?"

"You got my mail?"

He read Light his mail and wrote a letter for him, both Light and his parents still writing the same sort of things. Light pretended he was in a base camp and even talked of going swimming and eating ice cream. His parents, maybe lying too, said the fishing was good and his mother's heart was better.

"When are you going to kill the Tiger?" Jackson asked.

"When I get ready," Light said.

"The Tiger's killing men at the firebase. Are you waiting for him to kill Hale?"

"He won't kill Hale. Lifers like Hale never get shot."

Jackson learned from Light the Tiger had built sniping stations up in the tops of the big trees, the third canopy. He traveled from treetop to treetop by means of a system of Tyrolean traverses. The name sounded funny coming out of Light's mouth. Jackson guessed the army had taught it to him in reconnaissance school.

"When the air force drops napalm, he hides in a tunnel," Light said.

"Kill him tonight," Jackson said.

"My scope is fucked up."

"Broken?"

"No."

"Let me see."

Light shook his head and said, "There's weird shit in that scope. I told you I ain't using it no more."

Jackson remembered that first night at the firebase when he had seen the flash in the scope.

"I want to see," Jackson said.

Light blew out the candle. He took the lens cover off the scope and turned it on. A greenish glow appeared on the big end. It threw a circle of soft green light within the hut. Light squatted gook fashion and stared into it. He began to sway back and forth, mesmerized by the glow.

"Ain't supposed to be glowing. Nothing in it now. I don't want to see. Don't want to know who's gonna die no more." He continued, "One night a dragon'll jump out of it. I saw a dragon through it once over in the Ia Drang Valley."

"Loose wire, that's all," Jackson said, trying to remain calm.

Jackson wanted the scope back in perfect working order. A crazy Light might wander off into the jungle, never to return, his protection withdrawn. The Tiger would kill them all. Jackson hit the top of the scope with the palm of his hand. The glow disappeared.

Jackson said, "See, a loose wire, that's all. I'll tell Hale you want another one."

"No, don't want another starlight," Light said quickly.

"Kill the Tiger," Jackson said. "Do it now."

"Don't want to use the scope," Light said.

Jackson replaced the old battery with a fresh one and turned the scope on the jungle. He saw the trees through it clearly, like a forest growing beneath a green sea. Sparkles of light played around the outlines of the trees.

"It's working fine. You look," Jackson said.

Jackson started to hand the scope to Light, but he shied away from it as if Jackson were handing him a snake instead and shook his head.

Light said, "Remember the city I told you about. The mountain people say it's a temple city. Way up in Laos. No NVA, no American troops there. I could go up there and live. Never have to go back to the world."

Jackson gulped air.

"You can waste him easy," Jackson said.

"You do it," Light said.

Light attached the scope to the rifle and handed it to Jackson. The rifle felt heavy. Jackson knew he was not going to be able to shoot anyone with it.

"I don't know how," Jackson said, his breath beginning to come in ragged gasps.

"You walked up here tonight, didn't you?" Light said.

"Sure, but—"

"Not many men could have done it."

"You kept me safe."

"You found me, didn't get lost in the jungle. You're as good as the Tiger. He makes mistakes. Remember, he missed me."

Jackson pressed the rifle back into Light's hands.

"I can't do it. You know I can't. You waste him," Jackson said.

"Your daddy said he was proud of you in the letter. He won't be proud if you run away to hide in Laos. Remember your mother's heart. What if you stopped writing? It'd worry her sick. You could get killed up there and no one would ever know. Your folks wouldn't even be able to have a funeral."

"I ain't looking through the starlight," Light said.

"Then don't use it," Jackson said. "You're the best. Don't need a goddamn starlight to kill a dink sniper."

"I could use iron sights," Light said slowly.

"Right. Goddamn, it'll be fucking easy. Like hunting deer." Jackson took a deep breath and continued, "I'll help you. Just like we were on a deer drive back home."

"I need to think," Light said.

Light sat crosslegged in the center of the hut. What seemed like hours passed. Off in the distance Jackson heard the rumble of thunder. Light sat still, the rifle across his legs, his hands outstretched in front of him, palms up. Jackson, sitting with his back against one of the roof poles, tried to sleep, but the mosquitoes kept him awake. Finally Light spoke.

"You have to be the decoy."

"What?" Jackson asked.

"The decoy. You said I was the best. If I'm the best, then nothing's going to happen to you."

Jackson gasped for breath, thinking of the fiberglass duck decoys he used back home. Sometimes the decoys got shot too when the ducks settled down among them.

"Well?" Light asked.

"You tell me what to do," Jackson said.

"Right now we sleep. In the morning we kill the Tiger."

Jackson lay down on the dirt floor and closed his eyes. When he woke it was morning and Light was gone. Jackson hoped this meant Light had decided to go after the Tiger by himself.

He walked out of the hut and saw Light sitting on the ground tying off the top of a plastic sandbag cover with a bootlace. The outcropping was covered with a dense morning fog, so there was no danger of being seen by the Tiger.

"What you got in there?" Jackson asked, motioning toward the sack with the barrel of his rifle.

"Present for the Tiger," Light said.

There was a lump in the bottom of the sandbag cover. Maybe Light had frags or a claymore in it.

"What're you gonna do?" Jackson asked.

"Booby trap him," Light said. "You see, he'll be coming up to shoot at the firebase as soon as this fog burns off. We'll set you as a decoy. When he works around to get a shot at you, it'll be Christmas morning for the Tiger."

"Use the rifle?" Jackson asked. Light shook his head no, and Jackson continued, "What's in the sack?"

"Talking about a trap too much'll ruin it."

"It'd be safer with the rifle," Jackson said, beginning to wish he was back at the firebase.

"Can't see up into the top of the trees. Fucking trees are two hundred feet tall. Like trying to shoot squirrels hiding up in the top of a big cypress back home. Not the way to do it. Don't want to try to kill him in his house that way without the starlight."

Jackson followed Light into the jungle filled with fog. They walked slowly until they reached an especially large tree, which had buttresses at the base taller than Jackson's head.

"You go up," Light whispered in Jackson's ear.

"How?" Jackson asked.

Light took the barrel of his rifle and poked at something above their heads. A rope ladder fell to the ground.

"Known this was here all along," Light said.

Jackson was glad Light's confidence had returned, but he did not want to climb the tree.

Light continued, "You go up. Tiger's got a sniping platform. He'll know you're there. Only way he can get a shot at you is from another station on up the ridge."

"What if the trap don't work?"

"It'll work. Remember, you said I was the best."

Jackson put one hand on the first rung and hesitated.

"You scared of high places?" Light asked.

"I'm not scared," Jackson said.

Jackson started up the ladder. He had slung his rifle over his shoulder, barrel down. Every time he put his boot on another rung he felt it bumping against his back.

Don't look down, don't look down, he thought.

The climb was easy and soon he reached a bamboo platform in the crown of the tree. Below, the jungle looked like a deep, green sea.

Jackson waited for the fog to lift, but hoped it would linger on into the morning. He watched a set of ropes the Tiger had strung from another tree. The Tiger would come that way. Jackson imagined shooting the Tiger as the man came across on the ropes, and the thought of being the Tiger's killer excited him. He checked to make sure a round was in the chamber and set his M-16 on automatic.

Thunder rumbled over the mountains but the sun broke through the fog, and Jackson saw the sky covered with patches of clouds. He could see the firebase clearly. A tiny figure crossed the compound at a run and disappeared into a bunker. The big trees dripped water off their leaves. From the jungle floor, the smell of rotting vegetation rose up to him. A flock of birds settled in the branches above his head to scream at each other and drop twigs and pieces of fruit to the jungle floor. Along the curve of the ridge he could see holes that had been blasted out of the jungle by the bombing and treetops charred by napalm drops. Jackson pressed his back against the trunk and tried to breathe slowly.

Bark splintered off the tree next to his head as the shockwave of the bullet moved over him. The birds left the tree with loud squawks. An instant later Jackson heard the heavy report of the Tiger's rifle. Jackson threw himself face down on the bamboo platform, all the air temporarily gone out of his lungs, his whole body limp and heavy. But he managed to suck in several deep breaths and fire off a magazine on automatic in the direction the shot had come from.

Light's rifle cracked from the jungle floor up the ridge.

The Tiger shot another round at Jackson, the bullet clipping the toe of his right boot. Jackson pressed himself even closer to the platform and thought about jumping out of the tree. Light shot again, one round. The Tiger replied with two.

Then for a long time there was silence. The birds returned to feed in the branches above Jackson's head. Suddenly there were two simultaneous shots. Jackson listened hard to hear a body falling through the canopy. But there was nothing, only the cries of the birds circling over the canopy.

After waiting for what seemed like a long time, Jackson decided to try to go back down the rope ladder. If he could get off the platform, he would be shielded from the Tiger's fire by the trunk. He started to back off the platform.

Bamboo splinters flew up in his face, the sound of the rifle reaching him an instant later. The bullet had been deflected by the platform. Jackson pressed his face against the smooth, cool bamboo and gasped for breath. Light shot one round.

Jackson lay on the platform and waited. His body was covered with sweat, and the muscles in his legs twitched. Light and the Tiger still exchanged fire, the sound moving off farther up the ridge. Always there were two shots, one quickly followed by another. Then for a long time there was no sound at all. A troop of monkeys passed through the canopy above him. The birds returned. Jackson decided to try to leave the platform again. Light had fucked up, and Jackson no longer wanted to be a decoy.

He backed off the platform, moving very slowly and keeping his body pressed flat against the bamboo. When he was off the platform and shielded by the tree trunk, he breathed a sigh of relief. A pair of rifle shots came from far away, the sound muffled by the trees.

Jackson sat down with his back to one of the buttresses and tried to decide what to do. He thought of going back to the firebase. Light had almost got him wasted. A single shot came from even farther off in the jungle.

He stood up and after a moment's hesitation ran off in the direction of the sound. The Tiger would have a hard time hitting a moving target from the treetops, he reasoned. Twice he heard shots as he jogged through the forest, following a zigzag course on purpose, ducking behind trees, running at a crouch and all the time expecting to be shot by the Tiger at any moment.

There had been no more shots, and he wondered if the Tiger had escaped. Suddenly, someone reached out and pulled him to the ground behind a tree. At the same time the Tiger's rifle cracked from the treetops, the bullet making a splat as it hit the trunk.

"Keep your fucking head down," Light said. Then he paused and continued, "If this was night and I had the starlight, I'd have already wasted him."

"Goddamn, he almost got me. You said I'd be all right," Jackson said.

"You're still alive, ain't you? He was worried about me. Didn't

take the time he should've when he shot at you. Won't nothing
happen to you now either. Fooled me. Had another sniping station
I didn't know about."

"Let's get out of here."

"No, I got the trap waiting for him. We just gotta get him in the
right tree. Right now he's moving the wrong way. You stay here.
Every few minutes fire a few rounds up into the canopy. I'll go up
the ridge and drive him back where we want him."

Light left the cover and the Tiger tried a shot. Jackson noticed
the bullet did not even come close.

Yeah, Light'll waste that fucker, Jackson thought. Light's the
best.

Jackson stood with his back pressed against the tree trunk. He
held the M-16 on automatic around the side of the trunk and without
looking at his target fired off a magazine in the general direction of
the treetops. When he replaced the magazine with a fresh one, he
had trouble because his hands were shaking. He waited a few minutes and then did it again. Off in the trees he heard the crack of
Light's rifle. There was no reply from the Tiger's rifle, and Jackson
hoped Light had gotten him. Jackson watched the treetops, his neck
already sore from looking up.

Light joined him at the tree.

"We got him moving the right way now," Light said.

They followed the Tiger through the jungle. Light tried several
shots at him but missed. The Tiger shot back once, the bullet missing Jackson's head by inches.

"We got him now," Light said.

Jackson lay with his face pressed into the leaves and gasped for
breath.

Please, no more goddamn "Fish on the bank," Jackson thought.
I can't fucking take any more of this.

Then they lay in the bamboo thicket on their backs. Light watched
the top of a big tree. Jackson tried to follow Light's eyes up into the
treetops but could see nothing but a tangle of vines and leaves.

"Only way he can get a shot at us is from up there," Light said.
"He'll be where that big limb comes off to the right and forks."

Light pointed up into the tree, but Jackson could not even find the limb in the green tangle.

"Got him a bamboo platform built in the fork," Light continued. "I got the trap set on the platform. We'll see the branches move when he comes across on one of them Tyrolean traverses of his. Climb right over the trip wire. Won't see it. Be watching us. Think we fucked up, lying out here in the open."

Jackson did not like lying on his back, presenting his face as a clear target to the Tiger. A breeze stirred the leaves high up in the tree. Then Jackson thought he heard something moving in the treetop but decided it was only a bird. He looked for the rope, but could not find it. It probably ran across to the next big tree thirty yards away, their canopies interlocking. Once the Tiger had come across he would be almost directly on top of them, the bamboo no longer providing cover.

They waited. It was like squirrel hunting, only he did not have to worry about remaining motionless. They were the target, the bait. It was all right to move. Already it seemed like they had lain there for hours. Jackson listened to the sound of his own breathing, which to his surprise was smooth and steady.

The branches shook, no bird this time, but perhaps a monkey. Then Jackson heard the creak of ropes. He looked up into the canopy but could see nothing except the branches moving. Light waited, watching.

Don't let him find the wire, Jackson thought.

Jackson imagined at that moment the Tiger was getting ready to place one of those heavy, steel-jacketed bullets between his eyes. He looked at Light who still had his eyes fixed on the treetop.

Maybe he's going to let him shoot me, Jackson thought. But no, Light had it all figured out. The Tiger was finished. Surely the sack was filled with frags, the trip wire tied to a pinless frag resting inside a C-ration can, just waiting for the Tiger to hit the wire and pull it out. Yes, that was it, the sack was filled with frags.

Jackson sucked in great gulps of air, trying not to make noise when he did it. Trip it, trip it now, Jackson thought. He imagined the sack hidden in the leaves over the bamboo platform. It was a good trap except for the decoy part. The Tiger would not escape. Light looked at him and smiled.

Jackson thought about running, wondered what his chances would be. The next good cover was the trunk of the other huge tree, but he would have to run across thirty yards of open space, an easy target for the Tiger who might not even know they were there. Jackson concentrated on remaining very still.

The Tiger screamed. Jackson threw his hands over his head and pressed his face into the leaves to protect himself from the shrapnel. But there was no explosion. The Tiger came crashing down through the canopy. Light got up, and Jackson followed him.

A few feet from the body Light stopped. Jackson started to walk past him to get a better look at the Tiger, who lay face down in the leaves, but Light put out his arm and stopped him.

"Careful now," Light said.

Then Jackson saw it: long and green and thick as his arm in the middle, uncoiling itself from around the Tiger's neck. It glided away, disappearing into a clump of bamboo, green vanishing into green. Light turned the Tiger over, a man who was a little more stocky than was usual for the slender Vietnamese. The Tiger's neck and the side of his face were black and swollen.

"Face'll be blowed up as big as a watermelon and black as tar once the poison starts working good," Light said. "Had that bamboo viper hung on a bootlace and tied to a piece of bamboo laid across a forked branch. He hit the wire, pulled the bamboo off the branch. Snake dropped right on him."

"You're the best," Jackson said to Light, feeling like he was yelling "Amen!" with the people at home in church.

Thunder rumbled, and a gust of wind shook the canopy.

"Rains'll come soon. Hale won't have it so easy," said Light. "Don't worry. I'll be out here looking after you."

With Light in the lead, they moved down the ridge toward the hut. The thunder was closer now, and the sun had been swallowed up by the clouds, making it seem like twilight beneath the trees. Jackson was relieved that Tom Light the killer was back. No more spooks in the starlight scope, no more talk of going off over into Laos to live in lost cities.

Light led him back to the hut. Jackson sat on the ground exhausted. He looked at the toe of his boot where the bullet had made a groove in the sole.

"You take the starlight," Light said.

Jackson gasped for breath.

"I don't want it," Jackson said. "What would I do with it?"

"You keep it for me."

"You'll need it."

"I got the Tiger without it. They don't have nobody better than him."

Light put the scope in Jackson's hands.

"You ain't seeing the weird shit in it. You'll be all right."

Maybe it would be good to get Light away from the scope, Jackson thought. He didn't want Light to go crazy.

"We still got a deal?"

"Yeah, you write my letters. I'll keep you covered."

"I'll bring it to you when you want it back."

"Don't come 'less I call. I ain't killing no more. Dinks'll be moving out here. I got to know you're coming or they'll waste you."

Jackson put the starlight in his ruck and headed through the jungle toward the firebase. He wished he had not taken the starlight, which made a heavy lump in the bottom of his ruck.

CHAPTER

17

BEFORE JACKSON REACHED the firebase rain began to fall, the start of the northeast monsoon. He walked back through thick clouds that had dropped down over the mountain.

Jackson reported to Hale in the TOC.

"Light wasted the Tiger," Jackson said.

"Patrol reported the shooting. How come it took him so many shots? Thought Light was a good sniper," Hale said. "Where's the body?"

"Left him out in the bush."

"He won't get credit for that kill. Unless I see bodies, he won't go on R&R again."

Jackson wondered what Hale would say if he told him the reason Light had given up the starlight scope.

Hale went to work on his maps, and Jackson put his ruck under his cot. Then he squeezed the water out of his fatigues. It had been cold out in the bush, and he was still shivering. Labouf was asleep on his cot, having just come off a shift on the big radio. Jackson thought about waking up Labouf and telling him that he had Light's starlight, but decided against it. Labouf would probably want to start selling looks at it.

When Jackson lay down to sleep, every time he closed his eyes he thought of the weird things Light claimed he had seen through the starlight.

Light's going fucking bush happy, Jackson thought. Been out there too long.

But still he could not sleep. He got the starlight out of his ruck and, hiding it from the radio operator under his poncho, went out of the TOC. The rain had let up but the wind still blew steadily, bending the radio antennas on the TOC. Jackson climbed up on the sandbags.

He turned on the scope and looked at the camp. Everything seemed to be working all right. The bunkers were surrounded by sparkles of green light, and the raindrops made flashes across the scope. Jackson watched a soldier walk in from a bunker on the perimeter.

But when he turned the scope on the ammo bunker, he sucked in one deep breath and began to choke. On top of the bunker a tiny skeleton jumped about on the sandbags, waving its arms in the air.

"What the fuck," he muttered as he put down the scope and gasped for breath. Then he brought himself under control thinking, goddamn "fish on the bank."

But the tiny skeleton was still there, dancing frantically atop the bunker. Then the skeleton, its bones glowing in the dark, disappeared into the bunker. The spook had been much too small for a man, reminding Jackson of those glow-in-the-dark cardboard skeletons people put up during Halloween, except that this one had a tail.

Jackson walked slowly through the rain to the bunker. He tried to make himself breathe slowly but found it impossible.

Go back to sleep. Why're you going to look for something that's not there? he thought.

Then a voice sang, "If I don't need you no more in this world/I'll meet you in the next one and don't be late. 'Cause I'm a Voodoo Child/Lord knows, I'm a Voodoo Child."

Reynolds & Raymond, Jackson thought. Some of their crazy shit.

Jackson went into the candlelit bunker. Reynolds was playing his M-16. A monkey sat on Raymond's shoulder, the outline of a skeleton painted on his body with fluorescent paint. The monkey could not sit still, jumping about and waving its arms and legs. Then Jackson noticed the frag in the monkey's hand, one of the new kind shaped like a baseball.

"Sappers! Short-timer!" Raymond yelled.

Jackson watched the monkey pull the pin. The handle flew off with a clank, and the monkey tossed the grenade, the frag hitting the dirt floor with a thump and rolling toward him. Jackson started to run but tripped and fell, the clay wet and slick against his hands. Instead of the explosion, he heard Reynolds & Raymond laughing.

Raymond helped him to his feet. Reynolds replaced the handle and pin of the dummy frag. He gave it back to the monkey.

"Short-timer's a smart little fucker," Raymond said. "He'll scare the shit out of the dinks."

Short-timer jumped around the bunker, turning flips.

"Fucker's speeding," Raymond explained. "Loves the shit. Have to shoot him up twice a day."

"What happens when he gets hold of some live frags?" Jackson asked.

"Oh, he's been practicing with them too. Out on the perimeter. Needs to keep sharp. So we let him use one we took the detonator out of."

Jackson picked up the starlight scope. Reynolds quit playing his M-16.

"Let me look at that," Raymond said, stepping forward.

Jackson put the scope back under his poncho.

"That's Light's, ain't it?" Raymond asked.

"No, it's not."

"Sure it is. Alabama, you don't pull observation duty on the perimeter," Raymond said. "Don't need a starlight."

"Light wouldn't give up his starlight," Jackson said.

"You give it to us," Raymond said.

"Get your own."

"Alabama, we need the starlight to bring back Jimi."

"You are fucking crazy. I promised Light I'd keep it for him."

"Just let us borrow it."

"He didn't say anything about lending it out. You got to talk to Light. Ask him."

Reynolds had begun to play his M-16 again, Short-timer on his shoulder.

"How come you're still alive?" Raymond asked. "Other guys go out in the bush. They get wasted. Does it with the starlight. Fucking magic."

"Lucky," Jackson said.

Raymond stepped forward and put his hand on Jackson's poncho.

"Get the fuck away," Jackson said, shoving Raymond's hand away, holding onto the starlight tightly with the other.

Jackson started to back out of the bunker.

"We'll have that starlight," Raymond said. "Go ahead. Hide it. Sleep with it. Put it in the money man's locker. We'll find it."

Reynolds began to play his M-16 behind his back. Short-timer became excited and, jumping off his shoulder, began to turn flips.

Jackson left the bunker and ran toward the TOC, wondering where he could hide the starlight so Reynolds & Raymond could never find it.

After Jackson got back to the TOC, he wrapped the starlight scope in plastic to protect it from the water that had already begun to seep into the TOC and hid it under his cot. Hale had set a triple guard on the entrance and had threatened the guards with permanent duty on the fence if anyone, especially Leander, entered the TOC without his permission.

At least once a day Jackson checked to see if the scope was there. Then one night Jackson found the scope was gone, but no one had seen Reynolds & Raymond in the TOC. Jackson wondered if Labouf had discovered it. As he went to look for Labouf, he was met at the tower by Reynolds & Raymond. Light rain blew against his face.

"You take it back," Raymond said, handing the starlight scope to Jackson.

Reynolds played his M-16, and Short-timer sat on his shoulder with a frag in his hand.

"It's got the fucking strange shit in it," Raymond said.

Reynolds sang, "Well she's walking through the clouds/With a circus mind that's running wild."

"What strange shit?" Jackson asked.

"You seen it. That green light," Raymond said.

They walked away, leaving Jackson standing in the darkness with the starlight scope.

Jackson looked through the scope, sweeping it slowly across the camp. Everything appeared normal, bunkers, gunpits, and wire—all with that green undersea look to them, sparkles of light flashing around their edges. He lowered the scope and turned it over in his hands.

Reynolds & Raymond are fucking crazy, he thought.

Then the big end of the scope began to glow like a TV screen. Holding the scope in both hands, his back to the wind and rain, he bent over the starlight.

The screen grew brighter, but the green glow did not hurt his eyes. An image took shape. A soldier was in a small bunker, but who he was and what he was doing there was not clear. Swirls of green light flickered across the screen. Suddenly the soldier and the bunker disappeared in the flash of an explosion. The scope went dark. Then another image took shape and Jackson watched it all over again, this time looking closely, trying to identify the soldier and what he was doing. He decided it was someone manning one of the big starlight scopes or a radar machine. There were only a few of these, all facing the ridge.

Jackson returned the scope to its hiding place in the TOC and went to the perimeter.

The man operating the big starlight scope told him to get the fuck away and would not talk to him. Jackson hoped that he was going to be the one. The other starlight operator laughed at him when Jackson suggested that he might be safer out in the open. And the radar operator was up on speed, claimed he heard someone beating on a drum out in the scrub. Finally Jackson reached Alfred Ten-Deer's observation bunker.

"Alabama, you want me to put my radar on Tom Light?" Alfred asked and laughed.

No one called Alfred "Indian" or "Chief." Alfred seemed to be exactly the right name for him. He was quiet and polite and a good radar operator. He had been to college. Alfred was responsible for having given the firebase warning for several probes and one sapper attack.

"Alfred, you need to move your machine. I'll help you do it," Jackson said.

"Why? I got a bunker here. Good overhead cover. Don't leak much. It's fucking wet out there."

"This place is going to take incoming."

"The firebase? Light tell you that?"

"No, this bunker. Tonight, I think. Soon."

"Don't you know for sure?"

Jackson paused before he spoke, "I saw a man die in Light's starlight. You stay, you're gonna die."

"You see me?" Alfred asked.

"I couldn't tell for sure. You could move your machine."

"Alabama, you sound just like my grandfather with all that god-damn mystical shit. Old man thought he could talk to the spirits. Went out in the desert alone. Had visions. I think he was taking peyote."

"Alfred, I saw it in the scope."

"I heard all that shit about Light. He's a good sniper. Nothing more. You believe he can raise the dead with that scope?"

"No, but I saw a bunker take incoming. Look, R&R saw shit in it too. They're afraid of it."

Alfred laughed, "Those two are fucking strung out on speed. You seen that monkey they've taught to throw frags? Got him up on speed too. I wouldn't believe anything they say."

"I'll get the scope. I'll show you," Jackson said.

He went to the TOC and returned with the scope. When he turned it on, the end did not glow again. He pointed it at Alfred's obser-vation bunker, and the scope seemed to be working perfectly. Unless Alfred could see it too there was no use going out to talk to him. Jackson looked one last time. The big end glowed, and he watched a soldier die, but this time he was not so sure it was a man operating a radar machine.

Jackson walked across the compound toward the bunker line, looking for a bunker that looked like the one he had just seen in the scope. Suddenly mortar rounds started dropping. Jackson dived into the nearest shelter, a recoilless rifle emplacement. The firebase's mortars and 105s replied.

"Hey, it's fucking Alabama," a soldier said.

"Hale kick you out of the TOC?" another soldier asked.

"I—" Jackson began.

Rounds began to drop close to the emplacement and men scrambled for cover. Jackson heard the shrapnel whistle overhead.

"Get the fuck out of here, Alabama!" a soldier yelled. "You're drawing fire just like fucking Light."

The firing had stopped and someone shoved Jackson out of the emplacement.

"Go get somebody else fucked," a voice yelled after him.

Jackson ran for the radar bunker.

Alfred could still be all right. Maybe it was the next incoming that was going to get him, Jackson thought.

But when Jackson reached the radar bunker, he found the bunker had taken a direct hit which had collapsed the roof. A group of soldiers were already trying to dig out Alfred's body.

I don't want to know this fucking shit before it happens, Jackson thought, gasping for breath.

Jackson returned to the TOC and sat up on the roof for a long time in the light rain. Although he kept turning the starlight on, it remained dark.

After Alfred's death Jackson wanted to put the starlight away and never look at it again. He understood why Light wanted to get rid of it and how Light had known nothing was going to happen to him all those times Jackson had gone out in the bush to meet him. But other soldiers had died during the attack, and who was to say one of them, not Alfred, was the doomed soldier he had watched in the scope. The soldier might have died somewhere else, at Firebase Mary Lou or even over in Laos.

Yet every night, Jackson looked at the scope because he wanted to know what the future held for him. But he never saw himself in the scope, although he saw other soldiers die, always shadowy forms whose identities were uncertain. Jackson was sure he would recognize himself if he appeared in the scope. Jackson was never more afraid, choking and gasping for breath, than when he watched a doomed man's image take form in the scope.

But Jackson gave no more warnings. He had learned how useless that was by his experience with Alfred. He never knew for sure who was going to die. No one would believe him, and soon his reputation would be similar to Light's. Hale might banish him to the jungle.

Every night Jackson called Light on the radio but received no reply. He thought about going out to find Light but Light had warned him to stay at the firebase. Perhaps Light had seen something in the scope.

So Jackson kept watching men die in the scope, the starlight glowing the green light, the men's bodies torn by shrapnel or bullets, and as the glow faded and the screen turned dark, Jackson was left breathless and afraid.

CHAPTER

18

PATROLS BEGAN TO REPORT STRANGE SIGHTINGS out in the bush. They described a Buddhist monk dressed in yellow robes and carrying a rice bowl wandering about through the jungle. When pursued, the monk always disappeared into the trees.

Some of the men claimed the monk was real while those who had not seen him said he was a pothead's hallucination. Gradually as sighting after sighting was reported, most of the men at the firebase came to believe the monk was real. The men had begun shooting at the monk, and a pool was formed for the man lucky enough to kill him.

But there were those who claimed the monk could not be killed. The monk survived a direct hit with napalm and had been seen walking out of the flames into the jungle. The monk escaped after a Spooky had caught him in the open with its Gatling guns. Yet the soldiers who started the pool argued that the monk was just smart, a dink monk in the service of the NVA.

Then the NVA began to attack both the fence and the firebase again. During the firefights, the soldiers discovered the NVA refused to give up their dead, willing to take five or six casualties just to rescue one body.

After a rocket attack on the firebase, Jackson went up to the roof of the TOC to call Light. A steady rain was falling. He spoke Light's name into the handset over and over but received no reply, just the hiss of white noise.

"Tom Light, Tom Light," Jackson said into the handset one last time.

"I'm here," a voice said, coming not out of the handset but from behind him.

Jackson flinched and gasped for breath, smelling the jungle stink of Tom Light who stood before him, the rifle cradled in his arms.

"You got the starlight?" Light asked.

"In the TOC," Jackson said.

"You get it."

Jackson went into the TOC and returned with the starlight, careful not to wake Labouf who had just come off a shift on the big radio. Light put the starlight on his rifle.

"What you been seeing in the starlight?" Light asked.

"Troops getting wasted," Jackson said. "Am I going to be in there. Will you know? You look and see."

"I'll know."

"You know now?"

"Not until I see it in the starlight."

"You tell me if you see me in it."

"Nothing's gonna happen to you."

Light put the rifle to his shoulder and pointed it toward Laos.

"Fucking holy man is pressing me. Can't get him without the starlight," Light said.

Jackson said, "You'll waste him."

"Better than the Tiger. Different. Don't even carry a rifle. But he knows just like I do when I got the starlight."

"What's he doing out there?"

"Raising their fucking dead. Dinks almost got me last night. I kept killing them, but he kept raising. They brought him in 'cause of me."

Jackson sucked in a deep breath and said, "That monk can't raise the dead."

"Then why did I have to keep shooting the same fucking dinks over and over."

"How could you tell? It was dark. You didn't have the starlight."

"I could tell."

"Nobody can raise the dead."

Light had gone crazy, Jackson thought. But was the holy man raising the dead any crazier than the troops dying in the starlight scope before they died for real?

"Listen, young trooper, he can do it," Light said. "They brought him in to get me. Then they'll overrun this place. Won't be able to stop them."

"What are you going to do?"

"I'm gonna waste his fucking dink ass. I can do it with the starlight."

"Orange is young, full of daring/But very unsteady for the first go 'round," a voice sang.

Jackson watched Reynolds & Raymond climb up on the sandbags.

Reynolds continued to play his M-16. Short-timer rode on his shoulder holding the dummy frag in his paws.

"We been trying to get Alabama to bring us out to meet you," Raymond said. "You can bring back Jimi. Raise him right out of the grave. You can do it. Got the starlight. We'll take a month's leave. Fly back to the world and raise Jimi. We'll pay. We know where there's some money."

"Get the fuck away from me," Light said.

"Goddamn, you're the only one who can do it. You got the starlight."

Light said, "Can't do nothing with the starlight but waste troops."

"Dinks say you can," Raymond said. "You—"

Light swung the rifle barrel to point at Raymond's head. Short-timer jumped off Reynolds' shoulder and ran down the side of the TOC.

"You open your mouth one more time and I'll blow you away. Won't nobody be able to raise you."

Raymond took Reynolds by the arm and pulled him away. They

scrambled down the side of the bunker. Jackson heard the water splash beneath their boots as they ran across the compound.

"You wait for me to call," Light said.

Light left and disappeared into the darkness, leaving Jackson to sit alone in the rain.

Pictures in the starlight. Raising the fucking dead, Jackson thought. Crazy. All of it crazy.

Jackson did not have to wait long for Light to call. Two days later Jackson walked out the gate in a rain so hard he could see only a few feet in front of him and headed through the scrub for the jungle.

"I wasted the holy man," Light said as they sat together in the hut. "Got him and a dink suicide squad."

Jackson was surprised the leaf roof did not leak and the hut was not full of snakes and bugs. It felt much dryer than any bunker at the firebase. But the bunkers were not filled with that jungle stink of Tom Light.

Light explained how the NVA had come after him, led by the holy man.

"I kept wasting'em but he kept raising'em. Thought I was a goner," Light said. "Then I got a shot at the holy man."

Light had waited for them at a ford across a stream.

"They were dripping water, shining in the scope," Light went on. "First I wasted the dinks. Point man had a French submachine gun. Probably left over from Dien Bien Phu."

Light described how he had shot three of them in quick succession.

"They were dead, three head shots," Light said.

Jackson said, "Sure, you killed them like you always do."

"But I watched them get up," Light continued. "Known he's been doing it. But this was the first time I'd seen it. They were in the river. Running. Water spraying up all around them. Shining."

"Different dinks," Jackson said.

"No, the same. Same dink with that French gun. Don't see much of them MAT-60s no more."

"You missed."

Light slowly shook his head.

"Didn't miss," Light said. "I was fixing to shoot them again when the scope filled up with light, hurt my eyes. Light paused and continued, "Then I saw that old holy man with his shaved head and those robes. I put it on him."

Light put his forefinger on his left temple. "Shot him right here. Couldn't have wasted him without the starlight."

"You killed him," Jackson said quickly. "He's gone."

"I shot him," Light said. "It was like a big star cluster bursting all around me. I closed my eyes tight to keep them from getting burned. When I opened them and went to look for the body, he was gone."

"Did you see him get up?"

"No."

"They took him. If he could raise the dead, he would have raised himself. Think about it."

"Do you think they buried him?"

"Sure, in the jungle."

"Couldn't raise himself? Was just another good sniper? No different than the Tiger?"

"You killed three NVA, one Buddhist monk. The ones you saw in the river were different men."

Light nodded his head and seemed to agree.

"How did the big flare come out of him?" Light asked. "How did it get in me?"

Jackson said, "The scope. It's fucked up. Hale'll get you a new one."

"You saw the men die in the scope," Light said.

"I saw something. Don't know," Jackson said, gasping for breath.

The scope was dark, and Jackson began to wonder if he had gone crazy, if he had seen anything at all. He thought of Alfred Ten-Deer.

"I didn't see a goddamn thing in the scope. I lied! Nothing! Not a fucking thing!"

Jackson gasped for breath and could no longer talk. He grabbed Light by the sweater and shook him.

"You kill them all!" Jackson said.

"Waste them," Light said.

Light was shaking, his arms wrapped around his chest.

"Waste them, waste them, waste them," Light chanted.

He sat with his legs outstretched, the rifle lying across them. Jackson picked it up and looked through the scope. The trees were there in the weird green light. Nothing looked unusual. It seemed to be working perfectly.

"Works fine," Jackson said. "We won't see no more troops in it. We won't ever be in it."

"Holy, hooooly, hooooly man," Light chanted.

Jackson took a few slow deep breaths to try to calm himself. He put his hand on Light's shoulder. Light was still trembling.

"He was just some old Buddhist monk," Jackson said.

"Hooooooooly," Light moaned, his body still shaking.

Jackson put his arm around him. He felt like he had put his arm around a rotten log, Light's body damp and cold to his touch.

"You look through the scope," Jackson said, pushing the rifle into Light's hands. "There's no holy man in it now. You'll see."

Light shook his head and said, "Don't need to look. It's in me now. Flew out of him into me when I shot him."

Jackson removed his arm because Light had stopped shaking.

"What's in you?" Jackson asked.

"The power," Light said. "I can raise them. What am I supposed to do?"

"Kill the dinks," Jackson said.

"I don't know what to do. Just raise Americans? Raise the dinks too?

"You killed a Buddhist monk," Jackson said slowly. "He had a shaved head. Carried a rice bowl. Smelled like a goat. A priest, a man, just like us. The dinks buried him in the jungle. You waste the dinks. Keep me alive."

"No one has to die," Light said.

Light was calm now, his voice steady. Jackson began to gasp for breath.

"You're not Jesus Christ," Jackson said. "That dink monk wasn't Jesus."

"Didn't say I was," Light replied. "But the power came out of that holy man and went into me. I can feel it moving around."

Crazy, Jackson thought to himself. He's gone fucking crazy. Light talking like he was Jesus Christ.

"Why wouldn't the dinks give up their dead?" Light asked.

Jackson said, "They've always done that."

"No, they wanted the holy man to raise their dead."

What if? Jackson thought. But everyone knew the dinks did not think like Americans. Crazy. You'll end up talking like Light about raising the dead.

"I'll show you," Light said. "We'll kill us a dink, and I'll raise him just like the holy man used to do."

"Have you done it?"

"Not yet. I can do it. I can feel it in me."

What if he did it? Jackson thought. Would I believe then? Watch him touch a man and that man get up and walk away. No, Light's a good sniper. That's all. He's gone crazy.

"I believe you," Jackson said.

"No you don't, but you will," Light said. "You go on back now."

Light stood up and taking Jackson's arm pulled him to his feet and said, "I'll keep you safe."

"We made a fucking deal," Jackson said. "You keep my ass from getting wasted."

Light laughed. "If the dinks shoot you, I can raise you. I got the power."

Jackson was afraid Light would allow the dinks to kill him just so Light could raise him from the dead. A picture appeared in his mind of Light kneeling over his body and touching him over and over, trying to bring him back to life.

As Jackson walked back through the jungle, it was like the first night he had gone out in the bush, his breath coming hard and fast, every tree and bush that rose up out of the clouds threatening to begin walking in the night. He counted it as pure luck when he made it back to the firebase.

19

WHITE PATCHES OF FUNGUS began to grow on Jackson's armpits and crotch. Every day he peeled away strips of dead skin. Boxes of new uniforms were brought in every few days, and the men exchanged their rotted ones. At one end of the TOC was a seepage, and water dripped from the overhead cover into a puddle. Labouf was worried about mildew getting into his money.

"Jesus, we're setting the record for MIAs," Labouf said from his seat on his footlocker. "The general climbed all over Hale on the radio last night."

Jackson did not want to talk about MIAs and tried to change the subject.

"If we had a heat lamp, you could dry your money," Jackson said.

"Nothing will dry in this fucking rain," Labouf said.

They sat and listened to the drip. Jackson decided to let him talk.

"What's Light doing out there?" Labouf asked.

"Don't know," Jackson said. "Wasting dinks, I guess."

"The dinks don't seem to be paying much attention to him," Labouf said. "The slopes are kicking ass at the fence."

Hale had stripped the firebase of every spare man to reinforce the platoons on duty at the fence. Jackson noticed the NVA fought just as hard as before for their dead.

"Guys get wasted and when our guys go to look for them they don't find nothing," Labouf continued. "Weird shit. What do you think happens to those bodies?"

"Major Hale thinks the dinks are taking them," Jackson said.

"Fucking asshole," Labouf said. "The guys on the fence say that Buddhist monk's been taking them. But nobody has seen that fucker lately. Light say anything about that monk?"

"Light wasted him," Jackson said.

"I knew it," Labouf said. He laughed and continued, "That bastard won the pool. Probably don't even want the money."

"Light's crazy," Jackson said.

"Like a fucking fox. He's not going to die."

"I mean really crazy."

"How?"

"He says he can raise the dead. Says the holy man was raising the dinks. When Light shot him, he got his power."

Jackson stopped, breathing hard. After he calmed down enough to talk, he told Labouf about the pictures of the doomed men in the starlight.

Labouf said, "Goddamn, Alabama. Why didn't you tell me? Just can't recognize money staring you right in the face. Light's really got something to sell. I'm going to make some fucking money out of this. You'll see."

"You believe I saw troops die in the scope? You think Light can raise the dead?" Jackson asked.

"I don't believe nothing. But the men'll believe. They'll eat it up. Won't be able to give me their money fast enough."

"Light is fucking crazy," Jackson said.

"He's kept you alive, killed the Tiger, wasted the monk," Labouf said and then laughed to let Jackson know he was not serious. "Don't matter what we believe. It's not the dinks or that monk taking the bodies, it's Light. Everyone will believe he's raising them. We'll sell insurance to the troops. Say half their pay."

So Labouf started what he called his "Life After 'Nam" program.

"It's not right," Jackson said.

"Light's taking the bodies," Labouf said. "Maybe he can raise them. Who can say he can't?"

"That's crazy. That's what Light says."

"I know it's not the dinks who're doing it. What would they want with American bodies? Shit, Alabama, I know Light's crazy. I'm not dumb. Maybe he can't raise the dead, but he's kept you from becoming one of them. If any man could talk with the spooks, Tom Light would be the one."

"You're selling the men nothing."

Labouf smiled and said, "I'm selling them what they want to buy. It makes them feel better. You could say they're paying to keep the lines of communication open with Tom Light." Then Labouf asked, "You would want him to keep everybody alive?"

"Yeah."

"So nobody should complain. Light believes he's raising the dead. Those that pay'll believe it. Hey, won't a single customer complain."

"Leave me out of it," Jackson said, wishing he had not told Labouf about Light's craziness.

Labouf accepted only money orders or American dollars. The chopper crew chiefs bought them for the men in exchange for a commission. To Jackson's surprise most of the men signed up. Labouf told them they were to leave the dead out in the bush where Tom Light would find them after dark and raise them. The officers and some of the senior NCOs were the only ones who would have nothing to do with the scheme. And Leander, who said to Labouf, "Tom Light gets troops fucked. He don't save nobody." Then the engineers heard about it and Labouf did business with them. Soldiers continued to be reported as MIA. Labouf added more money to his footlocker.

The rains continued, the clouds often dropping down into the Cunt. And the rain gouged out gullies in the red clay which the enemy sappers used to approach the fence. The rain washed out the fence posts and flooded the underground bunkers so badly that on some days the men ended up perched up on top of them, exposed to fire from the enemy who remained hidden in the jungle.

Despite Labouf's "Life after 'Nam" program men still died. The men blamed these deaths on the officers who refused to let them leave the dead out in the jungle. They were convinced Light would honor his contract and as soon as it grew dark raise the men out of the bush. No one was quite sure where the dead went after Light raised them. Some said they went home, but others claimed they went to one of the R&R countries like Australia or Singapore.

The platoons at the fence continued to take casualties. Finally a man refused to give up a dead soldier to graves registration.

"Get your radio," Hale said to Jackson.

Jackson wondered if Light would also protect him from his own men. Luckily it was clear enough for the choppers to fly. The climb down the narrow trail to the Cunt was a difficult one. Jackson looked out past the door gunner and saw a group of men standing in a circle within a tangle of concertina wire.

When they reached the group, they found a man with an M-60 machine gun standing over a body bag.

"Pate won't give up Fernandez," a lieutenant said.

"Goddamn, Lieutenant, you're supposed to be in command here," Hale said. "You make that man put down his weapon."

"He won't, Sir. I already tried," the lieutenant said.

"Try again," Hale said.

The lieutenant walked over to Pate and said, "Soldier, put down that weapon."

"They're not putting Fernandez in the ground when he could live," Pate said.

Pate was a big man, and Jackson thought the M-60 looked like some child's Christmas toy in his hands.

"Soldier, your friend took a direct hit from a mortar," the lieutenant said. "There's just pieces of him in that body bag. Don't you think his family would like to bury him?"

Pate said, "Tom Light can raise him."

Jackson could barely hear the conversation because Hale had been gradually backing away from Pate and the lieutenant.

Hale looked up at the sky for a moment and then wiped the rain off his face. Jackson expected Hale might start screaming, but instead when the major spoke his voice was calm.

"Son, there's nothing we can do for your friend except give him a soldier's burial," Hale said, having to raise his voice to make himself heard since a good twenty yards now separated him from Pate. Jackson wished it was more. "He'll have an honor guard. He can be buried at Arlington if his family wishes. Put down that weapon. I won't court martial you. He was your friend. I understand."

"No, Sir," Pate said. "They'll take all the blood out of him at graves registration. Shoot him full of poison. It'll be too late for Light to save him then."

Pate motioned with the barrel of the machine gun at two soldiers who were standing off by themselves. They looked nervous, Jackson thought. Probably afraid the weather would get bad and trap them at the fence.

"You let me put him out in the bush," Pate said. "Tom Light will take care of him. Fernandez paid his money."

"You men are goddamn stupid to give Labouf your money," Hale yelled and took a couple of more steps backward.

Jackson began looking for cover.

Hale continued, "I can't stop you. It's your money."

"Tom Light won't let us die!" a man shouted.

"You show me one man he's raised," Hale said.

The men talked among themselves while Hale waited.

"He raises them out in the bush," Pate said.

"And where do they go?" Hale asked.

Pate said, "I don't know, but they live."

"I got a letter from Morrison," a soldier said.

"Yeah, show the major the letter," another soldier said.

The soldier produced the letter and handed it to Hale.

"This has an Australian postmark," Hale said. "This man is on R&R."

"He was MIA," Pate said. "How did he get to Australia."

"Who saw him get shot?" Hale asked. "Who reported him MIA?" The men talked among themselves but no one stepped forward. Hale put the letter in the pocket of his fatigue jacket.

"I'll find the real story on this man," Hale said. "Never was killed. Took an R&R to Australia and deserted. He's going to the stockade when the MPs find him. That man will be back doing his job on this fence."

Hale then took the lieutenant aside and talked quietly with him. The lieutenant kept shaking his head. Then the lieutenant walked to where Pate still stood over the body bag. It had begun to rain harder, and thick gray clouds dropped down over the firebase. The two men from graves registration kept glancing up at the sky.

"Soldier, for the last time I'm ordering you to put down that weapon," the lieutenant said.

Pate said, "I don't want to have to shoot you, Sir."

"But you could get that goddamn Tom Light to raise him from the dead if you did," Hale shouted.

By now Hale had to shout because he had backed off a good thirty yards.

"Soldier, if you don't put down that weapon, I'll have you shot," Hale shouted. "Lieutenant Sims will do the shooting. We'll zip you up in a sloppy rubber bag. You'll go on the chopper with your friend. The money you paid to Private Labouf won't do you any good. Even fucking Jesus Christ won't be able to do a thing for you once graves registration gets done with you." Hale paused and yelled to Lieutenant Sims, "Lieutenant, are you locked and loaded?"

Lieutenant Sims looked at his M-16 as if he was seeing it for the first time.

Hale continued, "I'm counting to ten. If that man has not put down his weapon by the time I reach ten, shoot him."

"One," Hale said.

By the time he reached five, Hale had backed farther away until he stood next to a foxhole. Jackson and the rest of the men moved away, everyone looking for cover.

"Eight."

Lieutenant Sims had still not raised his weapon. He appeared to have found something interesting on the receiver.

"Nine."

A soldier stepped forward and walked directly toward Pate. The soldier reached out for the barrel of the M-60.

"Ten."

Hale jumped into the foxhole, and Jackson stretched himself out in a puddle behind a pile of sandbags. When Jackson raised his head, Pate was sitting on the ground crying, and the soldier had the machine gun.

Jackson and Lieutenant Sims helped Hale out of the foxhole.

"What's your name, soldier?" Hale asked the man with the machine gun.

"Morrison," the soldier said.

Everyone laughed.

"You're supposed to be dead," Hale said. "You been writing letters from Australia?"

"Been right here," Morrison said. "Attached to the engineers up on Little Tit for a few days. Just got off the chopper."

Hale turned to the men. "You men want to believe a fucking hoax. Nothing'll help you except killing the enemy."

The graves registration team loaded the body bag on the chopper.

Hale took the machine gun from Morrison and raised it above his head and said, "This is the only thing that's going to keep you men alive."

Labouf became obsessed with signing up Leander in "Life after 'Nam." Jackson was sitting on a pile of sandbags by the TOC with Labouf when Leander walked by.

"It's not too late to sign up, Leander," Labouf said.

"Go talk your shit to somebody else," Leander said.

"Tom Light's been wondering why you haven't signed," Labouf continued.

Leander said, "I'll kill that motherfucker next time I see him."

Labouf laughed.

"No one can kill Tom Light," Labouf said.

"He got Calvin killed," Leander said. "Cost me a stripe."

Leander was now a corporal instead of a sergeant because of the short round.

"You got all these men believing that shit about raising the dead," Leander said. "I don't believe none of it."

"Just to be safe—" Labouf began.

"You go talk your shit to somebody else," Leander said. "Troops are still getting wasted. How come your protection didn't do them no good."

"You get a refund if you get killed," Labouf said. "Your family gets it. Like GI insurance. And the only reason anyone has to die is because the fucking asshole officers won't leave the dead out in the bush for Light."

"If I get wasted, it's only because it's my turn," Leander said.

He turned his back on Labouf and walked away.

Jackson tried to keep track of Light. During the day the tower guard reported that Light spent his time either in the hut or sitting in front of it in the rain. Jackson did not know what to believe. He did not want to go home crazy. Not end up like Light. Wandering through the jungle babbling to himself about the dead men he had raised. Now he was more afraid of Light than he had ever been, yet he knew he still needed Light's protection to survive the war.

Then Light called Jackson on the radio and asked him to come out. As Jackson walked through the jungle, he wondered if this would be the night when Light would decide to stop protecting him. The rain was falling very hard, and Jackson could see only a few feet ahead of him. As he came out of the jungle and onto the rocky outcropping, he saw a figure standing in the rain. At first he thought it was Light but realized the man was too big for Light, too big for a dink.

Jackson stopped and pushed the lever that put his M-16 on automatic. The man raised one hand, palm out. Jackson could see he did not have a weapon. Perhaps it was one of the listening posts who had gotten lost. The man motioned for him to come closer. Jackson walked farther out onto the outcropping.

It's Pate, he thought. No one at the firebase was as big as Pate.

But Pate was dead, killed three days ago in a firefight which had wiped out his entire squad.

"Jackson, you tell the major," the figure said.

Jackson was very close now, so close he could reach out and touch the man.

He's not real, Jackson thought.

"No one has to die," the figure said.

Jackson said, "You got lost. I'll show you how to get back to the firebase."

"I'm not coming back. I don't have to fight anymore. No one has to die."

Pate put out one of his big hands and placed it on Jackson's shoulder. The hand felt heavy and warm through Jackson's wet, cold fatigue jacket.

"You tell the major," Pate said. "You tell them all."

Pate turned and walked off, disappearing into the night.

Jackson found Light in the hut.

"Are you doing it?"

"What?"

"Raising them."

"Yes."

"I saw a man in the jungle. Did you raise him?"

"The big man? Yes."

"And the dinks?"

"Yes, them too."

"Where do they go?"

"Up into Laos. To the city. Where there is no war."

Jackson looked at the dark figure of Light and smelled that jungle stink. Like a skunk, Jackson thought. None of it made sense, but there it was. He had talked with Pate, touched him.

"We're both crazy, howling at the moon crazy," Jackson said.

Light laughed and said, "The war is crazy. We're not. Don't worry, I'll keep you safe."

Jackson wanted to watch Light do it, watch him touch a man whose guts had been shot out, watch that man get up and walk. But Jackson was afraid to ask.

"Come in, show Hale," Jackson said. "Men are dying every-day. Show him you can stop it."

"Tell Hale to leave them in the bush," Light said. "I'll raise them."

"What are you?" Jackson asked.

"Tom Light. Same as always. Son of a fisherman. Born poor, probably'll die poor."

"You're not Him come again?"

Jackson gulped air and waited for Light to reply.

"Why would He want to come back to this?" Light paused before he continued, "The power was in the holy man. Now it's in me. I don't know how. You come up to Laos with me."

"I want to see. There's no city," Jackson said.

Light turned on the scope. The big end began to glow with greenish light. There was the smell of electricity in the air. An image took form and Jackson crouched close to the screen. It was the city. Stone temples covered with vines. Soldiers, NVA and American, walking in a grassy parklike place. Women, children, playing on the grass.

I'm hallucinating, Jackson thought to himself. I'm going crazy.

He thought of Loretta, looked for her in the scope. The image faded and the electric smell in the air was replaced with the rotting leaf stink of Light.

Light said, "Nobody has to die."

"You come up to Laos with me," Light said.

"I want to go home," Jackson said, thinking of Loretta, thinking of the hundred days he had left.

"Come with me."

"No, goddammit, I'm going home."

"You look again."

The scope glowed, and Jackson saw mountains and a narrow valley covered with jungle. Then he realized it was Little Tit, Big Tit, and the Cunt. No sign of the fence, everything grown up. Not even a rusted steel post or a piece of wire showing.

"Before long there's not gonna be a fence or firebases," Light said. "You come with me."

Jackson looked in the scope again, the jungle smooth and uniform. Only the chopped-off tops of the mountains indicated that firebases had once been there. He looked for himself in the scope, wished he could know.

"What's going to happen to me? What if I stay?"

"If it's not in the scope, I don't know," Light said.

Jackson thought of the R&R he had taken with Light to Vung Tau and returned to find Hale's new RTO had been killed.

"No, I belong at the firebase," Jackson said, getting the words out all right but gasping for breath after he said it.

Jackson caught his breath and continued, "Remember we have a deal. You keep me covered."

Light said, "I ain't forgot. But you saw what was in the scope. You know what's gonna happen. Come up to Laos with me."

"I'll be all right. You keep me alive," Jackson said.

"You get killed I'll raise you."

"Shut the fuck up about that. You keep the dinks from wasting me."

"I won't go back on my word."

Then Jackson left Light at the hut and started back for the firebase. Light had promised, but could he trust a man who claimed he could raise the dead?

What did I see? Was it real? Jackson thought as he walked through the jungle. Alfred Ten-Deer had been real, no doubt about that. But that was not the same as raising the dead. By the time he reached the front gate, Jackson had begun to doubt again. No one had seen Pate die. Maybe he had survived the firefight. Pate's squad had gone out on a night ambush and vanished. Maybe Tom Light had found Pate and asked him to stay out in the bush.

And Jackson thought about the jungle-covered mountains and valley he had seen in the starlight. Then he considered returning to Light. He paused a moment before he continued to walk toward the firebase through clouds and a steady rain.

CHAPTER

20

THE NVA HIT LITTLE TIT with a night rocket and sapper attack in the middle of a heavy rainstorm. They breached the wire and ran through the camp tossing satchel charges. The rain and cloud cover made it impossible to call in gunships or fighters. Desolation Row gave them fire support along with the big guns from Firebase Mary Lou, but by morning the sappers had been reinforced by at least a company of NVA. The enemy hit the hill with rockets and mortars and began to push the engineers off. No one could see the battle because the mountaintops were shrouded in clouds.

Finally the engineers abandoned the mountaintop and retreated to the fence. Hale called in an arclight on Little Tit. The next day the air force blasted Little Tit, killing any NVA left on the hill and destroying the firebase.

Major Hale pulled the troops off the fence and assembled the men at the firebase. A gentle rain was falling, and clouds filled the valleys, the firebase like an island in a gray sea.

"Men, we're leaving this place," Hale began.

Everyone cheered. Hale waited until they were quiet before he continued.

"The enemy's been kicking our ass," Hale said. "Fence is going nowhere. We've been using the wrong tactics, that's all. General Morton has ordered us into Laos.''

"We're ready, Major," Raymond shouted. "We'll waste the dinks."

Reynolds played his M-16 with his teeth.

Jackson had been in the TOC when the call came through. Hale had protested that he was not ready, that he needed air support, but Morton had given him a direct order, leaving Hale no choice.

Hale took out a plastic-covered map and held it up for the men to see.

"I got air force pictures. If the dinks dig a goddamn new latrine at the Holiday Inn, I know. Dinks won't be expecting us, sitting over there fat and happy. Intelligence says there's about the same number of them as us. Thinks we might catch us a general if we're lucky. Remember, we'll have the element of surprise."

"Don't care how many of us die long as you make fucking colonel," Leander said, his pith helmet pulled down low over his eyes.

"Leander, you can get yourself plenty of those helmets where we're going," Hale said. Then Hale hesitated before he continued, "I didn't say it would be easy. Better than waiting for them to kill us here. Hiding underground like fucking rats."

"Fucking crazy," Leander shouted.

Hale ignored Leander and talked fast, "Men, we're going out in the jungle and destroy the enemy. The NVA will learn not to fight this unit."

Light probably gone off to Laos and now Hale deciding to get me killed, Jackson thought.

"We'll all get fucking wasted," a soldier shouted.

And another said, "I'm staying here."

The officers and NCOs went into the ranks to quiet the men.

"You will all go. You engineers are infantry now," Hale said, talking fast. "This firebase will cease to exist. We're not leaving a single goddamn C-ration can for the enemy to use. This mountaintop will be evacuated and bombed."

"I ain't going," someone yelled.

"Only way you men will get home is by way of the goddamn

Holiday Inn,'' Hale said. ''Next man opens his fucking mouth gets a court martial. You hear me, Leander?''

''Kill him now!'' Leander shouted. ''Kill the motherfucker.''

Two members of the mortar squad wrestled Leander to the ground. Hale continued, talking so fast now it was hard to understand him, ''Tear down the bunkers. Fill 'em in. Rip up the wire. Pull down the tower. Leave nothing for the enemy.''

Hale glanced up and down the ranks to see if anyone was going to challenge him.

Leander struggled with the men who held him. One held a bush hat over Leander's mouth. Jackson wished they would let Leander go so he could kill Hale, save them all.

''We're walking to Laos,'' Hale went on, calmer now but still talking fast. ''No choppers to let the enemy know exactly where we are. Slip up on'em. Won't build bunkers. Won't dig foxholes. No flak jackets or steel pots to slow us down. Leander'll be right at home with his fucking dink helmet.'' Leander tried to yell something but still had a mouthful of bush hat. Hale continued, ''By the time we reach the Holiday Inn, you men will be jungle soldiers. Learn to live and fight like the enemy. Be better than the fucking dinks.''

Hale dismissed the battalion. Jackson found Labouf in the TOC sitting on his cot staring at the footlocker.

''What am I going to do with it?'' Labouf asked, speaking in a whisper so the man at the big radio could not overhear.

''Send it to Saigon with one of the crew chiefs,'' Jackson said.

''They can't walk into the Bank of America with American dollars,'' Labouf said. ''I was planning on sending it home on a ship as hold baggage.''

They both stared at the locker.

''Maybe bury it,'' Labouf continued. ''But if we lose the war the North Vietnamese will never let me come back here. Arclight'll blow it to pieces.''

''You have to take the chance.''

''Yeah, no way to hump this money. No room in my ruck.''

In the morning, the footlocker was gone. Jackson did not want to know where Labouf had buried it.

They tore down the bunkers, emptied the sandbags, and used the dirt to fill in the holes. Even the piss tubes were dug up. A sky crane appeared during a break in the weather and removed the tower and the wire. They poured diesel fuel on the wood and sandbag covers and burned them.

The morning they left, Hale wandered about the firebase pointing out things the men had missed, like an empty sandbag cover or a set of rusty hinges off a mortar shell box. By the time the job was completed and the battalion walked off the mountaintop, nothing was left of the firebase but a field of red clay gullied by the endless rain, the filled-in bunkers marked by pools of water.

Jackson and Labouf stood looking at the muddy pool where the ammo bunker had been.

"Swimming pools for the dinks," Labouf said. "They'll like it here."

Leander walked up to them. Hale had busted him to private and put another man in his place.

"Labouf, folks'll be wanting their money back," Leander said. "Tom Light's still sitting in his hut. Bet he ain't going to Laos."

"He's going," Jackson said.

Leander laughed. "Glad I won't have to listen to no more crazy talk. Your man's shit is weak."

Leander walked off to help take down the mortars.

"Let me know how it feels humping tubes and baseplates over the mountains," Labouf yelled. "Maybe some slope'll put another hole in your fucking dink helmet."

But Leander did not turn around.

"He's out there," Jackson said, wishing the tower was still there so he could climb it and try to see Light's hut through the clouds and rain.

"Maybe," Labouf said.

"Dinks still won't give up their dead. They know he's there."

"Nobody's getting their fucking money back."

Tom Light, you better be out there, Jackson thought. Risked my ass to write your letters. Can't run out on me now.

The battalion marched past the fence in the Cunt, walking across the scrub toward the trees. Clouds filled the narrow valley and heavy rain fell, the worst weather the monsoon had brought so far. Even in the open it was difficult for Jackson to see the man in front of him.

In his ruck Jackson carried the radio, six batteries, six canteens, M-16 magazines, flares, smoke grenades, and three days' rations. He staggered under the load which felt like it weighed a hundred pounds, the straps cutting into his shoulders.

I had it made, Jackson thought. Light was my ticket home. Crazy goddamn bastard. Should've gone to the city with him.

He started to choke, his mouth wide open as he sucked in great gulps of air.

"Swallow a bug, Alabama?" a voice asked.

Jackson looked up and saw Labouf grinning at him. Labouf had been given the job of carrying an extra radio and spare batteries. His rucksack bulged with the load. He, like Jackson, was supposed to stick close to Hale.

Labouf continued, "We're fucked for sure this time."

Suddenly there was an explosion off to their right, followed by rifle fire and the chatter of a light machine gun, the fire close but the sound muffled by the rain. Jackson lay on the ground along with Labouf and Hale.

"Do something," Hale screamed into the handset.

"They're fucked," a voice came back, the lieutenant in charge of Alpha Company.

"A whole fucking platoon?" Hale asked.

Then the mortars started falling.

"Run for the trees!" a lieutenant yelled. "Everybody move."

They all ran, but Jackson knew the enemy was shooting blind. Only a lucky shot could get them. They entered the trees, the steady beat of the rain replaced by the irregular drip from the leaves.

Another machine gun opened up on them. Jackson lay with his

nose pressed into the leaves. He turned his head and saw Labouf lying beside him.

"Fucking Hale didn't have flank security out," Labouf said. "We lost thirty or forty men because of him."

Jackson subtracted that from the total. The addition of the engineers had given them almost five hundred men.

"Jackson, get me Charlie Company," Hale said.

Jackson spoke into the handset, surprised words were coming out of his mouth. He handed the handset to Hale.

Someone came running through the trees. Jackson threw his rifle up.

"Hold your fire!" a voice yelled.

Reynolds & Raymond dropped down beside them. Short-timer, his painted bones still showing, rode on Raymond's shoulder.

"We'll get'em for you, Major," Raymond said.

Reynolds sat up to play his M-16. Raymond pulled him back down. Then Reynolds switched on a small battery-powered tape recorder.

"After the jacks are in their boxes/And the clowns have all gone to bed," the voice of Jimi Hendrix sang.

"Cut that off, goddammit!" Hale shouted.

Raymond took the tape recorder away from him.

The machine gun was joined by another. Pieces of bark and bits of leaves dropped down on them as the gun traversed over their position. The battalion replied with grenade launchers.

"Short-timer'll get'em," Raymond said.

Jackson noticed for the first time that Short-timer wore a cloth vest in which he carried two frags. The pins had been straightened. Raymond held Short-timer on the ground, and the monkey squealed and twitched every time the gun tracked over them.

Raymond released Short-timer who immediately climbed the nearest tree.

"Tell'em to stop shooting. They get him all confused," Raymond said.

Hale gave the order over the radio, and the firing stopped. Jackson waited, pressing his body closer and closer to the earth, imagining the NVA creeping through the jungle now since the fire from the battalion had stopped.

Whaaamoom!

One machine gun stopped.

A few minutes passed and then Whaaamoom! the sound again. The second gun was silent.

Hale gave the order to resume firing.

But the NVA broke off the contact. Labouf believed they were falling back until the battalion reached a place where the enemy could be certain they could kill them all. The battalion had lost fifty men, among them was Lieutenant Sims. Also Morrison was now dead for sure. Jackson hoped that Tom Light was following them, raising the fallen men. There were a few wounded, but they could all walk. Heavy rain continued, and thick clouds dropped down over the mountains, making noon in the jungle appear like twilight.

The point squad kept making contact with the enemy. After a few hours only the squad leader was left alive. Hale replaced them with a fresh squad.

Labouf said as they took a break, "Won't be calling Phantoms or gunships in when we make contact. No medevacs. Nothing can fly in this shit. Don't get wounded so bad you can't walk. Gonna need more than a frag-throwing monkey."

Hale left a group of wounded behind with a medic and a squad for security. They were to call in a medevac when the weather cleared.

Where the fuck was Light, Jackson thought.

"I don't need air support," Hale said at a meeting of his commanders, which Jackson and Labouf as battalion RTOs attended. "The dinks don't have air support. We'll beat them at their own fucking game. Tell the men that anyone who falls out will be left behind."

"He didn't talk about the wounded," Labouf whispered to Jackson. "They're going to be left behind to die."

"Americans don't leave their wounded," Jackson said.

Labouf shook his head and said, "You wait. You'll see."

Please, don't let me get wounded, Jackson thought. Where is Tom Light?

Hale had continued his briefing, "And keep their goddamn feet dry. I don't want the whole battalion down with immersion foot." Jackson sloshed the water in his boots about with his toes and wondered how anyone was going to keep their feet dry.

"What about resupply?" a lieutenant asked.

"When we cross over into Laos," Hale said. "We'll need rations before the attack. If the weather is too bad for choppers to fly, we'll live off the land. There's deer. Wild pigs. Peacocks."

Off in the distance they heard a deep rumble.

"Arclight on Big Tit," Labouf said. "Hope they caught some dinks in the open."

If Labouf had buried his money on Big Tit, he did not seem to be concerned about it. Jackson imagined the bills floating through the air, blown out of their hiding place by the bombs.

Jackson kept expecting another ambush, but it never came. The rain continued. Although the big trees broke the direct force of the rain, there was the constant drip off the leaves. The men's boots stripped away the leaf cover, creating a slippery red clay trail to climb. Jackson pulled himself up the side of the mountain on tree limbs and vines. His body ached from the climb.

At night on laager, Jackson could count on only four hours of sleep because of guard duty. But his ruck was growing lighter because of the rations he had eaten. Some of the men had eaten almost all of theirs. Labouf had. "The place for rations is here," Labouf said, patting his stomach.

At noon of the third day Hale called a halt for a break and brought in his commanders for a conference. They huddled together under a bamboo lean-to covered with their ponchos. Labouf and Jackson sat in the rain with their backs to a huge tree, the vines wrapped around it larger than Jackson's leg.

"Do you think we're in Laos yet?" Jackson asked.

"Don't know," Labouf said. "I think dickhead Hale is lost. That's what they're doing now, trying to figure out where the hell we are."

"Where're the dinks?"

"Watching us. Waiting. Hit us when they're ready."

"Tom Light'll keep me from getting blown away," Jackson said.

Labouf laughed. "You said that fucker went crazy. How can you count on him?"

"The men keep sighting someone."

"Have you seen him?"

"No."

"It's dink scouts they've been seeing or hearing. Jesus, how could you see anything in this goddamn mess."

"Maybe Light's out there?"

Labouf laughed and said, "That's what I've been telling the guys who want their money back."

The officers were taking down their poncho lean-to.

"Time to start humping again," Labouf said. "They got my ruck so full of spare batteries I can hardly walk."

From Hale, Jackson learned the reason for the meeting. They were going into Laos. Hale had been worried that an ambush might be waiting for them when they crossed the border. Reynolds & Raymond had been sent out as scouts but had not returned.

"Where is it?" Jackson asked.

"Across the river," Hale said.

Hale had squads go out as extra flank security. The underbrush grew thicker as they came down the side of the mountain, the bushes and trees covered with thorns, making it necessary to cut a trail. Jackson heard the chink of machetes and knew the dinks could hear them too.

The jungle opened up into grassy fields along the narrow river which was almost out of its banks. Leaves, branches, and occasionally whole trees floated past. A light rain fell.

"We're going to drown in that fucking river," Labouf said.

Jackson did not see how they were going to get across, especially if the dinks were waiting on the other side. The river crossing was the perfect spot for an ambush. Then the squad walking point reported they had found a fresh trail in the tall grass.

"Dink ambush," Labouf said. "They'll squeeze us between the mountains and the river. Without air cover we're fucked."

The point squad followed the trail, moving very slowly because they were afraid of booby traps. Then they reported music coming from the edge of the river.

Labouf laughed and said, "The dinks listening to Saigon radio. Or fucking R&R."

Soon the squad called back and said they had found Reynolds & Raymond sitting by the side of the river listening to their tape recorder. The squad brought Reynolds & Raymond back to Hale.

"Where's that tape recorder?" Hale asked.

"We threw it in the river, Sir," the squad leader said.

Reynolds & Raymond looked like they had crashed and burned. Short-timer's fur was wet, and he no longer twitched and danced. He sat shivering on Raymond's shoulder with his arms around Raymond's neck. Hale gave them some rations and questioned them while they ate. Reynolds finished his can of spaghetti in several large bites and licked out the can like a dog.

"You seen any gooks?" Hale asked.

"Jungle's full of 'em," Raymond said. "Major, you take the battalion across the river and we're all gonna die."

"You hallucinated those goddamn dinks," Hale said in a loud voice. "If there were that many of then, they would've stayed and fought."

Raymond's hands trembled from fear or speed. Jackson wanted to ask them if they had seen Tom Light but decided to wait until later.

Reynolds was investigating Raymond's cans to see if any food was left.

That night the battalion went on laager in the field by the river. Reynolds and Raymond slept near Jackson in the center of the circle the battalion had made. Hale's orders were always the same. No digging. No talking or moving about.

When Jackson came off his watch, the rain had almost stopped, only a fine mist falling. There had been no probes of the perimeter or mortar attacks. Jackson heard Reynolds & Raymond whispering beneath a poncho. He crawled over to tell them to shut up.

"Not so loud. Keep your goddamn mouth shut. I hear you again, and I'll kick your fucking worthless ass," Jackson whispered, his face almost touching Raymond's. Short-timer began to chatter but Raymond shut him up.

"Short-timer wants some more speed," Raymond said. "But we got to conserve what we got."

Reynolds began to finger imaginary strings again.

Jackson grabbed him by the shoulders and shook him.

"I told you once to stop that, asshole," Jackson said.

Raymond said, "Leave him alone. I'll take care of him."

"Keep him away from me," Jackson said. "I don't want him to fuck up and get me blown away."

"You know what the money man did with his footlocker?" Raymond asked.

"Sent it to Saigon," Jackson said.

"Money man'd keep his money close," Raymond said.

"Shut the fuck up. What would you do with his money out here if you had it."

"He wouldn't have it then. We'd have it. Me and my buddy."

"Did you see Light out there?"

"No, and don't want to either. When you see Light, it means you're dead."

At the mention of Light's name Reynolds began to play his M-16.

"Stay quiet or we'll all be dead," Jackson said. "Keep him still."

Jackson returned to his radio and pulled the poncho over his head. He shivered in his wet fatigues which had already begun to rot, the cloth feeling slimy against his skin. The white fungus had spread to his legs and arms. It itched, and he tried to keep from scratching. Every night giant centipedes, five or six inches long, crawled into the poncho with him. They had a painful sting, and Jackson feared them more than leeches.

The rain began again, sounding like buckets full of pebbles were being poured on his poncho. He lay in an inch of water but was happy that at least part of his body was going to stay dry. Jackson looked forward to lying down in that cold water to sleep.

Before he went to sleep, he set the radio on Light's frequency. But after calling over and over and receiving no response he gave up. Light might be miles away, headed toward his abandoned city.

"Tom Light, Tom Light," Jackson whispered into the handset but received no reply.

He turned the radio off to save the batteries.

Get your shit together, Jackson thought to himself. Maybe Tom Light will save your ass. But if he doesn't you'll have to take care of yourself. Watch out for booby traps. Don't get wounded. Take deep breaths, slow now. Stay cool.

Jackson rested his head on his folded arms to keep out of the water and closed his eyes.

CHAPTER

21

HALE, JACKSON, AND A SQUAD LEADER CROUCHED in the grass by the river. The squad leader had a coil of white nylon rope slung over one shoulder. As they studied the river, the squad leader rubbed mud on the rope.

"Fucking rope," the squad leader said. "Everything in the army is green: tents, socks, jeeps. Why not OD rope?"

"Ask for a volunteer," Hale said.

The squad leader crawled off through the grass.

Jackson watched the river slide by, the surface littered with leaves and branches. He could barely make out the far bank through the rain and clouds.

The squad leader returned and said, "Nobody wants to go."

"Pick one," Hale said. "Do it quick."

"I'll go," Jackson said.

Hale said, "The dinks may be waiting on the other side."

"I want to do it," Jackson said.

Tom Light trying to keep you from getting wasted, Jackson thought. Why are you making it hard on him? Why can't you wait for the Holiday Inn? Plenty of chances then to risk your neck.

"Give him the rope," Hale said.

162

Jackson took off his clothes. The rain felt cold on his skin, the drops stinging when they hit. They gave him a .38 in a shoulder holster. He tied the rope around his waist and waded into the river. The water felt good, warmer than the rain. The water reminded him of the sea at Vung Tau.

"Don't try to fight the current," the squad leader said. "Swim straight across. Least they won't be able to see you in this shit. Not unless they're waiting on the bank."

As Jackson swam out of the bank eddy and into the current, he wondered what drowning in the river would feel like. If dinks were on the far bank, they would wait until he reached it before they killed him. His reward for carrying the rope across would be that Hale would expect him to swim the next river. Jackson was afraid but breathing easy as the current caught him.

Just like swimming the river at home, Jackson thought.

But as they paid out more of the rope, it bellied out, causing a powerful drag.

Stay cool. Keep swimming, he thought.

The current carried him fifty yards downstream before he reached the bank. Now the weight of the rope was dragging him back into the water. Jackson dug his feet into the mud and pulled to clear the rope which resisted for a few moments and came free. He tied it around a tree.

Then for the first time he was really scared. He gasped for breath as he took out the pistol and drained the water from the barrel and cylinder. While he lay face down in the grass, the point squad came over carrying just their rifles and ammunition. They went up the bank and established a perimeter so the rest of the battalion could cross safely.

Labouf joined him on the bank.

"You crazy fucker," Labouf said. "Don't you know not to volunteer."

"This white shit growing on me was itching. I needed a bath," Jackson said.

Labouf laughed and said, "You are a stupid dickhead."

"I did it," Jackson muttered to himself. "I really fucking did it."

Once the battalion was formed up again, they moved out slowly through the grass, taller than their heads and with sharp edges on the leaves that gave Jackson cuts on his hands.

Jackson heard the incoming at the same time someone yelled, "Mortars!"

He dropped to the ground, the ruck sliding forward and hitting him in the back of the head. More explosions followed and dirt fell on him. He flattened himself out, holding his hands over his head.

"Run, goddamn you!" he heard Hale shouting. "They got us bracketed. Run!"

Jackson did not think he would be able to get up and run, but when a shell landed close by, the shrapnel whistling through the grass and cutting down sections of it on top of him, he jumped to his feet and ran with the rest of the battalion.

The battalion ended up scattered in the treeline at one end of the field. Some had run the wrong way and gotten caught in an ambush. Jackson heard the machine guns and the men screaming for help. Finally squads and platoons formed up again. Jackson found Labouf sitting with his back to a tree.

Labouf grinned and said, "Hale just keeps fucking up."

Jackson located Hale who was talking with a medic. They stood over a wounded soldier, a member of the mortar squad.

We were lucky, Jackson thought. They could have killed us all.

"Call in a dust off," the medic pleaded. "This man don't have to die."

"They'll never be able to fly in this shit," Hale said. "Nothing but clouds and rain."

"We can talk him in," the medic said. "Those pilots are good. They'll do it."

"No time. We have to move," Hale said. "The dinks don't know which way we ran. They can't see in this shit either. They got lucky with the mortars. Heard us. I told that asshole lieutenant to keep his men quiet."

The medic said, "I'll stay with him. Leave me a radio. I'll call in a dust off when the weather clears."

Hale shook his head, "No, give him some water, morphine, rations, and a pistol. Tell him we'll pick him up on the way back."

"No, Sir, you tell him," the medic said.

They went through the trees and found a man lying on a poncho. A plasma bag hung from a limb, the bag connected to a tube stuck in his arm. Leander was going through the man's ruck. When Leander pulled out a lavender tie and tied it around the soldier's neck, Jackson recognized Marcus, the owner of the ruined suits.

"Foot's gone and shrapnel in the groin," the medic said to Hale in a low voice. "He's full of morphine. Right now he's stable. If you'd just let me call a dust off."

Hale went down on one knee beside the wounded soldier.

"Son, we're going on ahead to kick the shit out of the dinks," Hale said.

The soldier looked up at him with a vacant stare.

Hale continued, "We'll pick you up on the way back. There'll be a decoration for you."

"I don't hurt at all, Sir," the soldier said.

"That's good. Here's water, rations, more morphine," Hale said.

Hale took them from the medic and placed them by the soldier's right arm.

"Doc here says you're going to make it," Hale went on. "You hang on. Holiday Inn's not but a couple of klicks from here. Just over the mountain. We'll be back."

"You'll write home for me?" the soldier asked.

"You'll write them yourself when this is over," Hale replied.

Hale put his own pistol in the soldier's hand.

"Dinks come around you waste'em. Add to our body count," Hale said.

"I'll get'em, Sir," the soldier said.

"I'm staying," Leander said.

Hale walked a few yards to one side and Leander followed.

"Nobody's staying," Hale said.

Leander pointed to the wounded man and said, "We're all gonna end up like Marcus."

"Get back to your squad," Hale said.

Leander had his rifle slung over his shoulder, but Hale had a CAR-15 carbine in his hands. Jackson could tell Leander wanted to unsling his rifle. Hale knew it too.

"Call a dust off," Leander said. "You're fucking crazy to work without choppers."

"Soldier, you got yourself a court martial when we get back," Hale said.

"Won't be anybody coming back," Leander said. "Nobody to court martial. Nobody to press charges."

Leander kept running his fingers over the nylon rifle sling.

Trying to make up his mind, Jackson thought.

Hale said to a lieutenant, "Make sure that man gets back to his squad. You're responsible for him."

The lieutenant took Leander aside and talked quietly with him.

Leander started to walk off, but he stopped and pointed at the wounded man. "You'll pay for that, Major."

"Get him out of here, Lieutenant," Hale said.

Leander turned and walked off. Then they all went away, leaving the soldier lying on the poncho.

At noon when they took a break on the shoulder of the mountain, Jackson dropped his ruck and sat with his back against a tree. Labouf found him.

"Don't get wounded," Labouf said. "I listened for that pistol shot all morning. Heard it a dozen times."

"He'll do it when he runs out of morphine," Jackson said.

"Goddamn, shitty war," Labouf said.

Jackson wished Labouf would make a joke.

"I've been saving some pound cake," Jackson said. "You want some."

"Thanks," Labouf said. "There'll be no resupply now. It's going to rain like this forever."

Jackson opened the C-ration tin, and they ate the pound cake slowly.

"Army's got dehydrated rations. Got chili and chicken and rice. Good shit," Labouf said, his mouth full of pound cake. "Light.

Could carry two weeks of food easy. But we don't get the good shit. The motherfuckers in Saigon are probably eating them. All we get are these fucking C-rations.''

Reynolds & Raymond walked up. Short-timer looked like he was asleep, clinging to Raymond's neck.

"Gave him a couple of downers," Raymond said. "He needed the rest. Losing his fucking bones. Need to repaint them. Dinks think he's a fucking ghost. Scared shitless of him.''

"Goddamn, fucking speed freaks," Labouf whispered to Jackson.

Reynolds & Raymond sat down beside them.

"I told you to keep him away from me," Jackson said, pointing to Reynolds.

"He's cool today," Raymond said.

Reynolds sat perfectly still, as if in a trance, staring off into the jungle. Jackson noticed the man's eyes rapidly moving back and forth.

"You the money man?" Raymond asked Labouf.

Labouf continued chewing the last of his pound cake and said nothing.

Reynolds began to play his M-16 and sing softly, "There must be some kind of way out of here/Said the joker to the thief.''

Raymond touched the top of Labouf's ruck which was leaning against a tree.

"Get your fucking hand off," Labouf said.

Reynolds stepped back. Labouf swung the muzzle of his rifle on Reynolds's belly.

"You touch this ruck again and I'll kill you," Labouf said.

"Whatcha got in there?" Raymond asked.

Labouf said, "Same as you got in yours.''

"You know what he's got in there?" Raymond asked Jackson.

"Batteries for the radio," Jackson said. "Hale's making him hump extra batteries.''

"We'd carry some of them for him," Raymond said and laughed.

Reynolds sang, "There are many here among us/Who feel that life is but a joke.''

"I'll carry my own shit," Labouf said.

"We going to help you watch it," Raymond said.

"Stay the fuck away from me," Labouf said. "You're supposed to be out on recon."

All afternoon Reynolds & Raymond were never far from Labouf. They pretended they were walking flank security but always stayed only a few yards away, screened by the trees. Labouf threatened them, but they ignored him.

He's got the money in there, Jackson thought. They're going to get it.

The battalion went on laager that night on the side of the mountain. All night they were probed, and there was one mortar attack. More men died. No one got any sleep. Jackson tried to estimate how many men they had lost and decided they must have taken at least 150 casualties. But Jackson was almost too tired to count. He wanted to lie down somewhere and sleep for days.

In the morning, Jackson stood beside Hale as they got ready to move out. Reynolds & Raymond were there keeping track of Labouf. Short-timer was speeding again. He kept running up to the top of a tree and then back down again. His painted bones had faded further from the rain. Jackson wondered why none of the men were around. Hale noticed too.

"Where are the men?" Hale asked a lieutenant.

"Don't know, Sir," the lieutenant said.

"They walked on up the mountain," a sergeant said.

Jackson felt like Hale and his officers were all alone on the mountain.

They're going to frag us, Jackson thought, looking off into the trees.

Short-timer ran down the tree and over to Hale's ruck. The monkey reached his arm under the edge and pulled out a frag. Chattering and screaming, Short-timer ran to Raymond and climbed up on his shoulder.

"Don't have a pin in it!" someone yelled.

They all scattered. Jackson found cover behind a tree.

Someone had removed the pin from the frag and slipped it under

the edge of Hale's ruck. If Hale had picked up the ruck, the handle
would have popped off, and Hale would have died.

Carefully Raymond started to take the frag from Short-timer.

Reynolds was playing his M-16 behind his back, far gone on
speed.

Then Raymond had it, his fingers around the handle. Men came
out from behind trees.

"Green tape. Who's got some goddamn green tape?" Hale said.

Hale was so scared he was trembling, and his voice was shrill.

A lieutenant produced a roll from his ruck. While Raymond held
the frag, Hale wrapped the tape around the handle.

"What squad slept next to me?" Hale asked a sergeant.

"First squad, Second platoon," a sergeant said.

"Bring that squad leader to me," Hale said.

The officers passed the frag around while Hale waited for the
squad leader.

"We were fucking lucky," Jackson said to Labouf.

"Those that don't have to stay close to dickhead Hale are lucky,"
Labouf said.

The squad leader arrived, looking worried. Hale had one of the
lieutenants take the man's rifle from him.

"Who put it there?" Hale asked.

"What?" the squad leader said.

Hale held the frag under the man's nose.

"You knew it was there," Hale said. "That's why you pulled
out. Not a goddamn enlisted man within fifty yards of my ruck."

The squad leader glanced up at the trees.

Hale said, "Look at me, goddammit. You are responsible for
your men. Do you understand?"

"Yes, Sir."

Hale tossed the frag to the squad leader.

"Tie this to your ruck," Hale said. "You'll need it when we hit
the Holiday Inn. I see you, I want to see that goddamn frag. Sure
hope that tape doesn't wash off in this rain." Then Hale had the
lieutenant give the man back his rifle, and Hale continued. "Get the
fuck out of my sight."

The squad leader walked off into the trees holding the frag with both hands.

Hale picked up his ruck and gave the order to move out.

"Better forget about doing any more sleeping," Labouf said. "They'll try again."

I'm sick of it, Jackson thought. The dinks trying to kill me. Now I'm going to get blown away when they frag Hale.

Labouf continued, "Hale don't look like he's worried. Probably enjoys having his ruck booby trapped."

"Shut the fuck up," Jackson said, swinging his ruck up on his shoulders. "Just shut the fuck up."

Jackson turned his back on Labouf and walked away.

"You better loosen up," Jackson heard Labouf say. "The bad shit hasn't happened yet."

All morning Reynolds & Raymond shadowed Labouf. They gave up pretending they were pulling flank security and walked beside him, one in front and one behind, ignoring Labouf's threats. Finally Hale sent them out as scouts again.

The battalion reached a gap, a perfect spot for an ambush. They halted while Hale sent a platoon to scout it. Jackson sat down next to Labouf.

"You got a heavy ruck," Jackson said, putting his hand on Labouf's ruck. "I'll carry a couple of batteries."

"It's not heavy," Labouf said quickly.

"You got no batteries. Got it filled with money," Jackson said.

"You're crazy as R&R."

"Let me see?"

Labouf reached for his rifle.

"Gonna shoot me like I was R&R?" Jackson asked.

Labouf grinned and said, "Fuck it. Help yourself."

Jackson opened the ruck. Inside were bundles of money wrapped in plastic. Labouf kept glancing from side to side to see if anyone was watching them.

"Close it up," Labouf said. "Goddamn R&R are probably hiding in the trees."

"They don't need to see," Jackson said. "They know what's in here. They'll kill you for it first chance they get."

Labouf said, "Not those crazies. They're gonna get blown away scouting for Hale."

"So far the dinks haven't been able to kill them," Jackson said. Then Jackson paused before he continued, "Goddamn, Labouf, why did you bring it? Shit paper is all it's good for out here."

"I'm going home with this money," Labouf said.

"You see any place to buy a plane ticket?" Jackson asked.

Labouf said nothing.

"Sit there and count your fucking money," Jackson continued as he picked up his ruck. "I hope I'm not around when R&R decide to take it from you. Give it to them. Let them worry about it."

"I worked hard for this money," Labouf said. "Took plenty of fucking risks."

Jackson stood up, "Don't talk to me about your goddamn money. You don't care about anything but that money. I'm worried about getting fucking wasted."

"Tom Light's not going to let anything happen to you."

"He's gone fucking crazy! I don't even know if he's out there." Jackson stopped, gasping for breath.

"Take it easy," Labouf said.

Then Jackson walked off up the slope. When he looked back through the trees, he could see Labouf sitting beside his ruck, rifle in hand, staring off into the jungle.

Why didn't I stay with Light? Jackson thought.

Jackson concentrated on walking, making sure he planted each foot firmly in the rotting leaves before he straightened out a leg beneath the weight of the heavy ruck, one foot in front of the other, over and over. And his mind, numbed by the repetition, slipped into a daydream of walking the night jungle with the starlight, powerful and unafraid.

CHAPTER

22

EVERYONE HAD RUN OUT of rations, and there was no chance of resupply by air because the heavy rain continued, mountains and valleys both covered with thick clouds. Hale promised they were only a day away from the base camp. Jackson was hungry and thought more about food than he did about dying.

"The food is at the Holiday Inn. On the other side of this mountain," Hale said at a meeting of his commanders. "Dinks have got rice, fish, pigs. Good stuff. Kill them and take it."

"Sure, easy," Labouf said. "We been ambushed so many times I've stopped counting. How we gonna kill any?"

What was left of the battalion was strung out along the side of a mountain. The enemy kept up pressure against their rear and flanks.

Herding us like a bunch of goddamn cows, Jackson thought.

Hale had a count made and Jackson and Labouf added up the numbers that came in from the platoons. They only had three hundred men left. The rest were dead or wounded so badly they had to be left behind.

"The weather'll get better. We'll have air support when we hit the valley. Phantoms, gunships, and choppers for the wounded," Hale said.

172

"Won't see any Phantoms. This fucking rain will never stop," Labouf said.

Jackson wondered why the men did not mutiny. But if the men refused to go on the NVA would have a chance to mount an attack against a fixed target. And there was no chance at all of anyone making it back across the mountains with no rations and the NVA waiting at every likely ambush spot. Their only chance was the Holiday Inn and the air support which would come with a break in the weather. Jackson dreamed of choppers dropping down to lift them out of the jungle.

Then the NVA hit the center of the battalion with mortars and an ambush, the fire coming from the slope above them. Jackson and Labouf were near the front of the column with Hale. They ran to escape the mortars, moving forward and downhill to try to place a bulge in the mountain between themselves and the mortars so it would be much more difficult to bring fire on them.

Jackson stumbled through the trees, wishing he could drop the heavy radio so he could run faster. Rifle fire clipped the twigs and leaves around them, the bullets making little splats as they passed through the thick leaves. Then he lay with Hale and Labouf behind a big rock. Reynolds & Raymond, who were never far from Labouf, were there. Hale started to talk to his company commanders but dropped the handset and sat down with his back against a tree. For a moment Jackson thought Hale had been hit.

"You hit, Sir?" a lieutenant asked.

Hale shook his head.

The lieutenant handed him the handset. Hale pushed it away.

So the lieutenant took over. Charlie was all right but half of Alpha had been cut off.

Another lieutenant and a sergeant appeared. They talked together in a little group, all of them glancing at Hale from time to time.

"Major, two platoons of Alpha are cut off," a lieutenant explained to Hale. "What do we do? What are your orders."

"Goddammit tell'em anything you want. Why do I have to hold the hands of my fucking junior officers?" Hale said.

"They're dying! Do something!" the lieutenant shouted.

Hale sighed, "There's nothing I can do."

"Do you want me to take command of the battalion?" the lieutenant asked.

"Fuck no! This is my fucking battalion!" Hale shouted. Then he continued in a calmer voice, "I'll command a brigade before I'm through. This battalion's going to the Holiday Inn."

Hale got up and after taking a compass bearing walked off into the jungle. They all followed.

"This time it ain't a couple of squads or a platoon. There's at least a fucking company of those dinks on this mountain," Labouf said. "Where's fucking Light?"

Jackson had been thinking the same thing. Light would not have to kill anyone. He would just have to show up and the NVA would scatter.

You bastard, you better keep my ass covered, Jackson thought.

The lieutenant continued to talk on the radio to the two platoons. Finally he told them that no one was coming to help them, that they would have to fight their way out of the trap on their own.

"Shoot that bastard, Hale!" the voice came out of the handset. "Call in choppers. Get us out of here!"

Then they heard the RTO trying to make contact with a Forward Air Control plane. Suddenly the radio went dead.

"Those platoons didn't react properly," Hale said. "We move when the enemy ambushes us. Let themselves get pinned down."

Jackson wondered if the lieutenant was going to shoot Hale, but instead the man got up and walked off.

"Let us put Short-timer on those dinks," Raymond said.

Short-timer chattered and turned flips, the bones on his legs almost faded away.

Reynolds held his M-16 like a guitar and pulling the trigger down fired off a whole magazine into the air, dancing and twitching in rhythm to the sound.

"Goddamn, get those fucking crazies out of here," Hale said. "I want both of you out ahead scouting. I want to know about the next ambush before it happens."

They were able to break off contact with the NVA, but they all could hear the fire from the two trapped platoons as they walked through the jungle. Now the battalion was under no one's particular command. The lieutenants asked Hale for orders, but all he would do was give them the compass bearing for the Holiday Inn.

"Fucking idiot. Throwing those men away," Jackson heard a lieutenant say to a sergeant.

They came to one of the many streams that cut the steep mountainside. It was not deep but flowing fast. Reynolds & Raymond were waiting for them at the bank. They had not crossed. The sounds of Alpha's firefight, although faint, still reached them.

"Cross over," Hale said to Reynolds & Raymond.

"Good place for an ambush," Raymond said.

Hale said, "Get over there, Labouf."

"Let the crazies go," Labouf said.

"You, now," Hale said.

"Well, fuck it," Labouf said and waded into the stream, his legs spread wide apart to brace himself against the current.

"Easy," Labouf said turning back to talk to them. "Dinks are still fucking with Alpha."

Then there was a heavy sound like a car going past on the highway. Labouf was suddenly lifted into the air. He dangled just above the surface of the stream, the heavy clay ball studded with punji stakes sticking into his ruck.

"Jesus, help me!" Labouf shouted.

Labouf had tripped a wire set in the stream, and the ball, which was attached to a rope, had been released.

"Get me down you dickheads!" Labouf screamed.

Everyone laughed, even Hale.

Reynolds & Raymond waded into the steam and helped Labouf out of his ruck. The force of the studded ball had been absorbed by the ruck, and Labouf was unhurt.

They helped him out of the stream, and Jackson checked Labouf's back. One punji stake had barely broken the skin. A trickle of blood ran down his back, but Labouf was all right. A medic dusted the wound with sulphur powder.

"Hey, leave that ruck alone," Labouf said to Reynolds & Raymond who were pulling the ruck off the punji stakes.

Labouf started back out into the stream but stopped when Reynolds & Raymond managed to pull the ruck free.

Hale decided he wanted to talk with one of the platoons. But Jackson had trouble making contact, the signal fading.

"Put in a new battery, Jackson," Hale said.

"Used the last one yesterday," Jackson said.

"Get one from Labouf," Hale said.

Labouf was in the stream, struggling with Reynolds & Raymond over the ruck.

"Get those batteries over here," Hale said.

Labouf fell down in the stream, and Raymond brought the ruck to the bank.

Raymond stuck his hand through one of the holes the punji stakes had torn in the green nylon fabric and pulled out a plastic-wrapped stack of bills. Labouf scrambled out of the stream and, jerking the bills out of Raymond's hand, stuffed them back into the ruck.

"Look at that fucking money," a lieutenant said.

Everyone except Hale and Jackson crowded around the ruck.

"Leave it the fuck alone," Labouf kept saying. "It's mine, goddammit. It's mine."

They pulled all the money out of the ruck.

"Shit, there must be a hundred thousand dollars here," the medic said.

"Labouf, where are those fucking batteries?" Hale said.

Everyone got quiet.

Labouf said nothing.

"Get Alpha on Labouf's radio," Hale said to Jackson. And to Labouf, "You fucking idiot! What'd you do with the batteries?"

Labouf looked up into the treetops.

"Threw'em away. You goddamn bastard! You'll go to jail for this," Hale said.

Hale pointed his carbine at Labouf and said, "I should shoot you myself."

"You better save your ammo for the dinks," Labouf said and grinned.

Jackson could not make Labouf's radio work.

Hale said, "Get the battery out of it. Put it in yours."

Firing started up not far away. An element of Charlie had made contact with the enemy.

"Quick!" Hale said.

Jackson opened the radio. Instead of a battery there were bundles of money. Labouf had even removed the radio itself and filled the aluminum case with money.

"You go find me some batteries," Hale shouted at Labouf. "Move!"

Labouf ran off into the jungle.

Hale picked up the ruck and threw it into the stream. Money scattered everywhere. They all scrambled for it while Jackson and Hale watched. Everyone got some, but Reynolds & Raymond retrieved the ruck and got most of it.

"Got the money man's stash. Gonna buy me a Cadillac back in the world," Raymond said.

"There are many here among us/Who feel that life is but a joke/Said the joker to the thief," Reynolds sang.

The firing still continued. Then the mortar squad brought their mortars in on the enemy and the fire stopped.

Labouf returned with two batteries, and Hale was able to talk to his commanders.

Hale had everyone return the money to Labouf. Reynolds & Raymond grumbled but handed it over.

"You're going to carry this money. Hump it all the way to the Holiday Inn. Maybe the dinks'll have a big PX where you can spend it," Hale said. "You and those two crazies are going to be my scouts from now on."

Labouf did not complain. He seemed happy to have his money back.

They crossed the stream. Far off on the mountain, Jackson could still hear the fire from the two trapped platoons.

Luck been keeping me alive, Jackson thought. Just like Labouf. Nothing but luck. Light on R&R in some fucking lost city. Then Jackson decided he no longer cared. It did not matter that he was wet and tired and hungry. Now he hated the dinks who had killed so many of them. He wanted to see the Holiday Inn. Run yelling with the other men as they made their assault on the bunkers, waste the dinks. Make them pay.

CHAPTER

23

BY THE TIME IT GREW DARK the battalion had broken off contact with the NVA. They wandered on the mountain, directed by the lieutenants who conferred with Hale before making any decisions. Occasionally they could hear the distant sound of firing from the two trapped platoons. Instead of stopping for the night, they kept moving. Hale never gave the order, but no one mentioned stopping. Once they reached the valley they had a plan, the details known to everyone from Hale's briefings. Jackson supposed the plan was the reason they kept moving, that and the chance to be airlifted out of the valley if the weather cleared.

"He's getting us to a place where the dinks can finish us off," Labouf said.

Labouf had survived a day with Reynolds & Raymond. He had come in to report to Hale and receive his instructions for the night.

"Maybe it'll clear and we'll have air support," Jackson said.

"Alabama, you're the only one in this whole battalion who believes that shit," Labouf said.

They reached the crest of the mountain and started down the side. This was the first time the battalion had been on the move at night. Jackson kept tripping over vines and walking into limbs, and he wished he had Tom Light to lead him through the jungle. Soon Jackson began to hear the faint sound of drums and gongs along with shouts and chanting. From Hale's briefings Jackson knew there was a Montagnard village at the foot of the mountain. The people of the village served as porters for the NVA and grew food for them.

"Goddamn funeral the Yards are having will distract the enemy," Hale said to a lieutenant. "Maybe the dinks'll be drunk on rice wine too. Most of them will be fucking base camp soldiers. Gone soft. Easy pickings."

"They'll be waiting for us," Labouf whispered to Jackson.

Then Labouf went out to scout ahead of the battalion.

Where was Tom Light? Jackson wondered.

Hale's plan of attack was to advance between the village on their right and the paddy fields on their left across the valley of scrub and grass. A creek ran down the center of the mile-wide valley. The larger bunkers were located on the far side at the foot of the mountain, but there were small bunkers and trenches scattered through the scrub between the creek and the mountain. According to intelligence, most of the NVA were across the border in Vietnam. Hale wanted very much to capture the general who made his headquarters at the base camp.

"Most of 'em are still up on the mountain looking for us," Hale said. "We lost 'em in the dark. The rest are tied up with those two platoons from Alpha. Had it planned that way all along."

The battalion slowly moved into a position at the foot of the mountain and waited for dawn. From a few yards in front of where Jackson lay next to Hale came the sound of falling water which Jackson supposed was a small waterfall made by a stream running off the mountain. Except for an occasional shout, the village had been silent for several hours. Then it stopped raining, the trees still dripping on them. A water buffalo bellowed, a rooster crowed.

Sounds just like home, Jackson thought.

The sky began to lighten.

"It'll clear. We'll have air support," Jackson heard Hale whisper to a lieutenant.

Jackson watched Hale take the silver eagles out of his ruck.

"Put'em on for me, Jackson," Hale said.

Jackson started to pin the first one, but Hale's fatigues were rotten and the cloth disintegrated beneath Jackson's fingers. Finally he found a spot that held and attached the eagle. Then he pinned on the other one.

"One battle away from these," Hale said.

Hale had Jackson put on the whip. After several unsuccessful attempts, Hale managed to make contact with a Forward Air Control plane. The one battery they had left was getting weak. Air control promised Phantoms if the cloud cover over the valley lifted and, later, helicopter gunships and medevacs. Hale had Jackson radio this news to all his commanders.

As it grew light, Jackson saw the waterfall was water from three six-inch-thick bamboo pipes the Montagnards had driven into the hillside, the water falling into a large pool which had formed below. Around the pool the grass had been cropped short by the hill people's livestock. Jackson held a flare and waited for Hale's order.

Jackson pressed his face down into the leaves, smelling that Tom Light stink. Hale tapped him on the shoulder, and Jackson raised his head.

"Get ready," Hale whispered in his ear.

Then Jackson saw a figure at the pool, a young Montagnard woman. She wore a piece of shiny black cloth wrapped around her from her breasts to her ankles and carried a small baby on her back. The woman took the baby out of the sling and placed him on the grass. Then she unwound the cloth and taking the baby in her arms stepped into the pool.

Hale was looking at his watch. Jackson wished he had the starlight so he could know if he was going to live. Light knew. Where was he?

The young Montagnard woman bathed the child who began to cry as she splashed water on him. Then she bent over and placed him on her back. The baby lay his head to one side and stretched out his arms to cling to her. Keeping the child balanced on her back, she began to bathe herself. Just then the sun cleared the mountains and through a break in the clouds fell on the pool, the light shining off a brass ring the baby wore around one ankle.

Loretta, Jackson thought.

He imagined how it would feel to hold her again, and he felt himself grow hard.

"Do it now," Hale whispered.

Jackson rolled over on his side and, aiming the flare at a thin place in the tree cover, started to hit the bottom of the tube with his palm. But he hesitated, glancing at the woman who was still in the pool. She had begun to sing, her voice soft.

"Now!" Hale said.

Jackson hit the tube, the star cluster going off with a pop, the flare ripping through the leaves, taking forever to clear the trees. But finally it did, and with another pop the parachute opened, and the red flare began to burn. As Jackson scrambled to his feet, he saw the woman with the baby in her arms staring up at the flare. The baby looked at the flare and laughed. She started to scream, her mouth opening wide, but he heard no sound coming out because the shooting had started—frags, automatic rifles, machine guns drowned out the woman's screams. Leander's mortar squad began to fire at the bunkers.

They were all up and running. Jackson's legs were not working right, for it seemed to him that it took minutes instead of seconds for him to run past the woman who crouched with her screaming child by the side of the pool, the mother trying to wrap the piece of cloth back around her body. Her breasts, big with milk, swayed as she tugged at the cloth. The baby reached for her, one tiny hand clutching a breast. Finally they were past the woman and her baby, Jackson looking for cover as they ran into the village, but forced to go where Hale went because Hale had the handset in his hand.

Then enemy mortar rounds began to drop on them. Hale yelled orders into the handset, calling on platoons that no longer existed and commanders who were dead.

Good cover over there in that ditch, Jackson thought. Hide behind that bamboo. We're fucking exposed.

Jackson wanted to turn around and run back into the jungle. Find Light. Go to the city.

But Jackson had no other choice but to follow Hale past the huts. One was on fire. Suddenly two soldiers only an arm's length in front of them were cut down by a burst of AK-47 fire. Jackson could see the bullets hit, the impacts spraying water off the men's uniforms and the sun forming rainbows in the spray for a brief instant. Then they were in a ditch, Hale lying beside him. Jackson gasped for breath and raised his head to watch, but all he could see was a burning hut and a dead American soldier lying on his side curled up like he had lain down to sleep in the sun. Most of the soldier's back was missing, the muscles and ribs visible.

I'll look like that, Jackson thought and tried to force the thought of his own death out of his mind.

Jackson began to shake and gulp air.

Why not me? Jackson thought. Tom Light's not here. Luck. Nothing but fucking luck.

"Goddammit, keep'em moving," Hale shouted into the handset to a platoon from Alpha that was still trapped back up on the mountain. "Keep'em spread out. Don't bunch up."

"They're up on the mountain," a lieutenant said.

"Why aren't they down here? They'll all get a court martial!" Hale screamed.

Someone silenced the enemy rifleman with a grenade launcher.

"Not much resistance," Hale said to a sergeant. "Few strays in the village getting some Yard pussy."

They passed the village, the battalion spread out through the scrub. So far the resistance they had met was not that of soft base camp troops. Even single men had stood and fought until they were killed. And the battalion was taking casualties.

Then a pair of Phantoms appeared, dropping down into the valley with a great roar. For an instant they seemed frozen over the valley as Jackson looked at their markings and the pilots under their canopies. The ground shook from the impact of 250-pound bombs, and Jackson pressed his body close to the earth. Suddenly they were gone, kicking in their afterburners with a roar and climbing almost straight up into some scattered patches of cloud that were beginning to move in. They made three passes, dropping bombs and napalm in the field and at the foot of the mountain where the main bunkers were located. Jackson was close enough to the napalm drop to feel the heat from it. Everyone cheered. Jackson yelled too. He wanted the Phantoms to cover the valley with napalm, fry the dinks.

Hale talked to the pilots on the radio. They complained that the NVA had placed the bunkers at a place against the mountain that made it difficult for the planes to negotiate the narrow valley and drop bombs on them. They made a final run and were gone.

Under the cover of the airstrike, they pressed on to the creek and forded it. Jackson had been wondering when the helicopter gunships would show up and a medevac for the wounded, but now blue-black storm clouds had blocked out the sun, and pieces of cloud had dropped down into the valley. Soon they would be fighting in the rain. He imagined flying out of the valley on a chopper. If only one came, Hale would end up on it and he would go too as Hale's RTO.

"Hold off," he said softly to himself. "Give us two hours."

Forward Air Control called and told Hale they would have to withdraw the fighters because of the bad weather that was moving in. No choppers would be coming unless the weather improved.

Jackson wondered how it would be if Tom Light could really do it. Light walking about after the battle, raising dead soldiers with a touch of his hand. Crazy, Jackson thought. Fucking crazy. You've been lucky so far. Maybe it was never Tom Light at all. Just luck.

Then they met their first real resistance. At least a platoon of NVA were dug in. Leander brought his mortars in on them but as soon as the rounds stopped, the guns out of ammunition, the enemy was firing again. The NVA mortars at the bunkers were now getting their range.

Under the direction of the lieutenants they sidestepped the pocket of resistance. Now instead of standing and fighting until they were killed, the enemy began to fall back.

"Goddamn they're falling apart," Hale shouted into the handset. "Try to take that fucking general alive."

Jackson had never seen Hale so excited. But Hale was careful to direct the battle from the safety of a ruined bunker, the overhead cover blown off by a 250-pound bomb leaving only a pit, the grass around it burned black from a napalm strike. Part of a sandbag wall was still in place. The charred bodies of the dead NVA had been frozen by the napalm in the positions they had died and looked like grotesque mannequins. The smell was very bad. Troops directly to their front began firing LAWs at the bunkers.

"Kill'em, kill'em, kill'em," Jackson repeated over and over.

Suddenly they began taking light machine gun fire from both flanks. The gunners were in no hurry. They took their time, making sure every inch of the field was covered. Mortars followed. Jackson crouched against the clay wall of the pit while he listened to Hale scream at his commanders.

No one will ever find our bodies, Jackson thought. The jungle will eat us. We'll rot. In a week there'll be nothing left. Light! Where the fuck are you?

Now the rain fell harder and thicker clouds moved in, making it impossible for Jackson to see more than a few feet. Figures ran up out of the clouds, and a lieutenant dropped into the bunker beside them.

"Goddamn double envelopment," the lieutenant said. "Center collapsed and sucked us in. Trick's older than the fucking world. There's a goddamn brigade in here. We need an air strike so we can break out."

Hale got back on the radio and began trying to contact Charlie and Alpha. But he received no reply.

"Dead, wasted," the lieutenant said.

Then one by one and in small groups the remainder of the battalion found their way to the pit and formed a perimeter around it. The man with the frag wrapped in green tape was there, the frag now almost the size of a softball from the extra tape wrapped around it. Then Labouf and Reynolds & Raymond jumped into the pit. Shorttimer still rode on Raymond's shoulder. Everyone else had dropped their ruck, but Labouf still wore his.

Labouf looked quickly around him and said, "Alabama, let's get out of here."

"How? They got us surrounded," Jackson said, willing to listen to anyone's plan for escape, no matter how crazy.

"They won't get my money," Labouf said.

Jackson then knew Labouf had no plan.

"All the money man's got is money," Raymond said.

Leander jumped into the pit beside Hale.

"Where's your fucking battalion, Major?" Leander asked, the pith helmet strapped tight under his chin.

Hale had lost one of his silver eagles. He sat in the mud at the bottom of the pit with his back to the wall.

"You better get rid of that dink helmet before somebody shoots you by mistake," Hale said.

"Fucking Major Hale. Got my men wasted so he could make colonel."

But Hale had stopped listening to Leander. He was looking at his map.

Instead of firing his M-16, Reynolds played it and sang, "I want to take you home, I won't do you no harm/You've got to be all mine. Foxy Lady."

Leander loaded a new magazine into his M-16 and began to fire over the side of the bunker.

"Come on, Major! We gotta fight. Ain't no use looking at a map!" Leander shouted.

Jackson stood up and began to fire off into the rain and clouds.

Suddenly Leander sat down, his helmet spinning off his head into the mud. He fell backward and hit with a splash in the water that had begun to collect in the pit, lying face down in the mud. The helmet now had two bullet holes in it.

That'll be me. That'll be all of us, Jackson thought.

"Come on, Alabama, let's get out of here," Labouf said as he stood up. "We can make it."

"No, don't go," Jackson said.

Labouf scrambled up the side of the pit. Jackson tried to stop him, but Labouf pushed him away. Then Jackson slipped in the mud and fell. Jackson got up in time to see Labouf run a few steps and jump into a bomb crater occupied by the man with the frag wrapped in tape. Mortars began to drop in on them, and just as Jackson put his head down, he saw Labouf and the soldier disappear in a cloud of smoke. When he looked up again, individual bills floated down like rain, and bundles still wrapped in plastic bobbed in the water at the bottom of the pit.

"Money man lost his money again," Raymond said.

Reynolds & Raymond began to scramble to pick up the money.

"Goddamn dinks!" Jackson shouted.

Jackson sucked in great gulps of air and fired his M-16 off into the clouds.

The lieutenant left the pit to take command of the men on the perimeter, taking everyone except Reynolds & Raymond and Jackson with him. The NVA were squeezing them, closing the circle.

Raymond said, "We'll send Short-timer out, Major. He'll kill the dinks."

Short-timer's bones had almost completely faded away. Raymond straightened out the pins on two frags so Short-timer would have an easy time pulling them out. Then he placed the frags in Short-timer's vest.

"Go get'em, Short-timer," Raymond said.

Short-timer was speeding again. He turned a couple of flips and chattered. Then he pulled the vest over his head and dropped it in the water. Short-timer jumped out of the pit and disappeared in the grass.

"Hey, you fucking deserter! Come back!" Raymond yelled and fired off a burst after him.

"No need for a fight, Major. We'll buy'em off," Raymond said to Hale.

Hale sat in the mud at the bottom of the bunker, and covered his face with his hands. He pulled off his remaining silver eagle and dropped it in the puddle of muddy water at his feet.

"Fucking conscript army. Professional troops would've taken those bunkers," Hale said.

Jackson grabbed Hale by the front of his fatigue jacket and shook him. Then he shoved the handset in Hale's hand, but Hale refused to take it.

"Get us out of here. Call in choppers. Get the Phantoms back," Jackson said.

Hale said, "No use. They won't come." Then he paused and continued. "Who would want to live in a fucking country where it rains all the time?"

Jackson called the Forward Air Control plane.

"Negative, Freight Train," a calm voice said, the only one Jackson had heard all morning. "Hold your position. Wait for the weather—"

But the last of the man's words were lost in a buzz of static. The battery was almost gone.

"We can't hold. Goddamn, drop it on our position," Jackson said.

"We can't copy. Say again," the controller said.

"On our position," Jackson said.

Jackson picked up Hale's map out of the mud and gave the controller a set of coordinates.

"We do not copy. Say again," the voice said, this time very faint.

Jackson threw the radio into the water.

"Tom Light! We had a goddamn deal!" Jackson shouted.

"Where's Tom Light?" Hale asked.

Jackson said nothing.

Hale shouted, "I'll have his ass court martialed. He'll learn to wear a uniform."

"Light ain't here, Major," Raymond said. "We'll get us out of here."

"Be decorations. Soldiers like you. Backbone of the army. Professionals," Hale said, talking very fast, running the words together.

Reynolds & Raymond gathered up more bundles of money and climbed out of the bunker.

"Hey you fucking dinks," Raymond yelled. "Buy yourselves some Cadillacs. Buy a new tank for mama-san. Case of frags for baby-san."

Reynolds & Raymond began to throw bundles of money off into

the grass. A burst of automatic rifle fire came from the grass. Raymond went down. Then Reynolds. Jackson fired off an entire magazine on automatic in the direction of the fire.

Jackson looked around. The bottom of the bunker was covered with dead soldiers, only he and Hale left alive. Hale sat in the same position, his back against the wall. The rain was rapidly filling up the pit.

"Major, we've got to get out of here," Jackson said.

"Call in an arclight. Bombs. Goddamn dicks. Kill'em all," Hale said, talking so fast now Jackson could barely understand him.

"No time for an arclight," Jackson said.

The rifle fire had almost stopped. Jackson stuck his head cautiously over the edge of the bunker. A soldier dressed in a pith helmet and green fatigues ran across an open space and jumped into a bomb crater. When a second soldier ran across the space, the man running in what seemed to Jackson like slow motion, Jackson shot him, the dink collapsing with a groan. The man moved, and Jackson emptied the rest of the magazine into him.

"Major, should we surrender?" Jackson asked.

Jackson's hands shook as he loaded a new magazine.

"Never surrender. We're getting out of here," Hale said.

Hale jumped to his feet and started to climb out of the pit.

Jackson pulled at Hale's fatigues, but Hale turned his rifle on Jackson.

"You mutiny, I'll kill you!" Hale shouted.

The major climbed out of the pit, paused, and fired a burst from his M-16 into the grass. It was answered by AK-47 fire, and Hale collapsed.

Jackson was alone.

Goddamn you, Tom Light, we had a fucking deal, Jackson thought.

Jackson heard the NVA yelling to one other as they closed in. He decided to surrender. No point in resisting any longer.

Mortar rounds began to fall, the gunners walking them toward the pit. Closer and closer they came, the shrapnel whistling overhead until Jackson decided they had rounds in the air that were going to fall into the pit. Jackson started to scramble up the side, but as he put his hand on a sandbag, a great sound filled his ears. He was falling, but he felt no pain. Then he heard himself hit the water with a splash. He could still see and think. He was not dead. But when he looked down he saw his intestines had fallen out of his stomach. They were shiny and wet looking. He reached down carefully and tried to put them back in. They were wet and slippery and hard to handle, kept falling out of his hands. He worried about the rain falling into his open belly. He smelled his own feces.

I don't want to die, he thought. Not here. Not like this. Tom Light, you bastard.

Then he succeeded in pushing the intestines back into his stomach and placed his hands over his belly, spreading his fingers to keep them from falling out again. Jackson felt a great sense of relief. Still there was no pain.

He looked up a saw and little man dressed in a green uniform and wearing a pith helmet standing at the edge of the bunker. Jackson searched for his rifle with one hand and could not find it. Instead his hand closed around what he thought at first was a piece of shrapnel, but it was too smooth for that. When he raised it out of the water, he saw Hale's silver eagle in his hand.

The NVA soldier had a frightened expression on his face, his mouth open, revealing a gold tooth. He carried his AK-47 with the muzzle pointed at the ground. Then the man's expression changed to a grim, frightened look like he had come upon a dangerous animal like a snake and the soldier brought the barrel of his rifle up.

Jackson raised one hand while keeping the other on his stomach.

"No, don't," Jackson said.

Someone yelled in Vietnamese to the soldier who looked over his shoulder. Then the man ran, not bothering to look at Jackson again.

Jackson saw another figure appear at the edge of the pit. It was Light, standing there with the rifle cradled in his arms. Light started down into the pit.

"You bastard, you lied to me," Jackson said.

As Light bent over him, Jackson tried to speak, to curse Light, but could not. And then the rain and the clouds and the stink of his bowels and Light disappeared.

CHAPTER

24

JACKSON OPENED HIS EYES. The sun was shining. He lay on the grass beneath a banyan tree, the grass smelling like his father's pasture in the spring, fresh and clean and new. The grass, waist-high, stretched away with clumps of trees and bamboo scattered here and there. Above the trees rose stone temples with trees and vines growing out of the crevices between the weathered stones. Beyond the city were green mountains covered with clouds, and the sun was setting behind them, the light shining on the temples.

Tom Light, cradling the rifle in his arms, walked into Jackson's field of vision. Jackson felt dizzy and weak, barely able to focus his eyes on Light.

"Where am I?" Jackson asked.

"My city," Light said.

Jackson felt his belly, the skin warm and smooth beneath his fingertips.

"Come," Light said.

Jackson touched the scars again expecting to wake from this dream to find his intestines in his hands, blue and slick and full of shrapnel holes. Light's figure went out of focus again. When Jackson opened his eyes, he expected to find himself with Light in some jungle

191

clearing. Instead he saw the ruined temples and Light squatting gook-style with the rifle across his knees.

"Where's Labouf? Where are the men?" Jackson asked, looking at his belly now, the skin wrinkled from the rain but unbroken. It was all too real to be a dream. He remembered the feel of the intestines beneath his hands.

"I ain't raising no more. You're the last one. I kept my word," Light said.

"If I'm a ghost, how come I can feel my heart beating?" Jackson asked.

"You ain't a ghost," Light said.

They entered the city at twilight, the sun disappearing behind the mountains. Monkeys climbed about over the stone temples, most of the carvings of animals and humans so worn and faded that Jackson had no idea what they represented. But he did recognize the carving of an elephant carrying men into battle and a human figure with six arms.

Light stopped at a plaza paved with stones. He took the starlight off the rifle and turned it on, placing it in Jackson's hands. Then Light walked away, Jackson hearing the pat of Light's sandals on the stones. Jackson felt cold and traced his scars with his fingertips. The starlight glowed with green light and an image took shape.

"Loretta," Jackson said.

She was walking across the big yard toward his parents' house. Jackson could smell his mother's roses. Loretta stopped and turned to face him. He reached out for her and pulled her away from the porch, out onto the grass beneath the pecans.

"Loretta, Loretta," he said, pulling her close to him, unbuttoning her clothes but at the same time knowing she could not be real, that all this was a dream, and when he woke it would be to the terrible pain of a belly wound. Perhaps Light had given him morphine, all this nothing more than a morphine dream.

He felt her close around him soft and wet, and he did not care if it was a dream. The cicadas whined above their heads in the pecans.

"Loretta, I'm home," he said.

"Don't leave me again," she said.

He shuddered atop her, and it went on and on, the warmth draining out of him, Jackson thinking that if he held onto her tight enough, he would never have to leave her. But he felt her slipping away. The green light was fading. Trying to hold her was like trying to embrace a pool of green water. "Loretta!" he cried.

Jackson found himself on the plaza again. Light stood watching him. He gave Light the starlight.

"You can stay here," Light said.

"We had a deal. You said you'd get me home."

"I raised you."

"Should've kept me alive."

"Nobody leaves this place."

Jackson started to gasp for breath but managed to control himself and speak.

"Don't want to spend my time looking at spooks in the starlight!"

"You leave and you're on your own."

"Better than staying here."

Light paused before he spoke.

"All right. I'll take you to Firebase Mary Lou. You live. You die. It's up to you."

"You look in the scope. Tell me what's gonna happen."

"You ain't in there now, but you could be later."

"Leave. Come with me."

"Can't. I'm staying here."

"I'm leaving. I'm going home. You take me to the firebase."

"We can be there by morning if we move fast."

He followed Light out of the city into the jungle, wondering what it would be like to spend the rest of the war without Tom Light but most of all dreading the moment when the morphine would wear off and the dream would end. Light had given him an M-16 and two bundles of Labouf's money still wrapped in plastic. Jackson wished Light had raised Labouf. As they walked through the rain and clouds, Jackson considered all the ways he could die and at the same time thought of life in the temple city. Maybe that was what Light was offering, a permanent morphine dream. All night they walked, mostly along the ridges. From time to time Jackson stuck his hand under his fatigue jacket to make sure the wound had really disappeared. He still kept expecting to wake up and die.

"We're close now," Light said as he called a halt in a narrow valley.

"Come with me," Jackson said.

"Can't leave. I belong at the city."

"Your parents?"

"I'm MIA. I'm dead."

Jackson took Light by the shoulders, Light's body wet but warm through the sweater, that rotting leaf stink on Light again. Light was no ghost either.

"Go home to Loretta," Light said. Then he continued, "Mary Lou is over the next ridge. You can find it easy."

Light walked off into the jungle. Jackson wanted to call out after him. He shivered from the cold and took a deep breath before climbing back up into the mountains.

Instead of walking to Firebase Mary Lou, Jackson planned to follow the mountains to coastal plain. Walking for real or in a dream, it didn't matter.

He might not see another person until he came down from the mountains. No Vietnamese lived in the mountains, only the Yards. The Vietnamese were smart, left the malaria and the tigers and the leeches and the snakes to the Yards. Jackson moved easily though the jungle, the leaves wet against his face, the constant drip from the huge, vine-covered trees rattling against the leaves. He looked up, the drip wet against his face, the tops of the trees lost in the low clouds which hung over the mountain. And he was afraid, the trees and vines forming a green net over him. Not the gasping, choking, "fish on the bank" panic this time, but something worse, deep within him, chilling his bones. Not the fear of death, but the fear of being alone, lost in the green sea of the jungle. He ran a hand over his belly—still smooth and warm and alive.

Don't let me wake up, he thought, wondering if he was pleading with God, Tom Light, or the jungle itself. Please don't let me wake up. Let me keep dreaming if this is a dream.

But this was no dream, Jackson thought, the rain wet on his face, the wet air heavy in his lungs. Light was the dream. He remembered how Light had walked off, the jungle closing around him. Light might build a hut near one of the temples, his clothes rotting away, no one to talk with, only the ghosts of the men he had imagined he had raised. Light had raised no one, all of that a crazy dream. One day the battery would run down, and the starlight would go dark. Too late for Light to go home. No place for him but the city of ghosts.

Crazy, fucking crazy, Jackson thought.

Jackson touched his belly with his fingertips, traced with them where the scars should be. Yes, he would walk to the sea, walking at day and night also. Maybe he would come upon a Yard village where he could buy food. If not he would live off the land. Food was everywhere: snakes, insects, grubs under rotten logs, fish in the rivers. Light had lived that way. Maybe he would get lucky. The next ridge might be one that ran all the way to the sea.

Once at the sea he would follow the coast to Vung Tau, walking on the white sand by the blue water. At Vung Tau he would hire one of the fishing boats to take him out to the line of freighters. Then he would buy passage home, standing on the deck and watching the green mountains fade and disappear as the ship carried him out into the South China Sea.

SCOTT ELY served in Vietnam from 1969 to 1970. He received an M.A. from the University of Mississippi and an M.F.A. from the University of Arkansas. Mr. Ely lives with his wife and children in Arkansas, where he teaches. He is at work on another novel.